The Key with Hearts

Hearts in Hazard ~ Book 9

By

M. A. Lee

WRITERS INK BOOKS

Published in the United States of America

Cover Illustration by Deranged Doctor Design

www.writersinkbooks.com

winkbooks@aol.com

Acknowledgements

My especial thanks to my family, who kept the beasts at bay during the writing of this novel.

To **Deranged Doctor Design**, creators of inspiring covers that keep me writing.

Novels by M.A. Lee

12 Books of the Hearts in Hazard series
A Game of Secrets
A Game of Spies
A Game of Hearts

The Dangers of Secrets
The Dangers for Spies
The Dangers to Hearts

The Key to Secrets
The Key for Spies
The Key with Hearts

The Hazard of Secrets
The Hazard for Spies
The Hazard with Hearts

Into Death ~ Post World War I
Digging into Death
Christmas with Death
Portrait with Death (coming soon)

Non-Fiction Works

Think like a Pro Writer series
Think like a Pro ~ 1
Think / Pro: A Planner for Writers ~ 2
Old Geeky Greeks: Write Stories with Ancient Techniques ~ 3

Discovering Your Novel ~ 4
Discovering Characters ~ 5
Discovering Your Plot ~ 6
Discovering Your Author Brand ~ 7
Discovering Sentence Craft ~ 8

*Just Start Writing ~ **Inspiration 4 Writers** :: book 1*

Table of Contents

1813

Chapter 1

Friday, 3 September

Myers Montford manor and estate in Wiltshire, England

The little dog nosed along the edge of the bricked planters. His white tail wagged, excitement quivering through his whole body. He sniffed at every speck, dirt and leaf and twig. Brightly colored ribbons, tied tightly together to create a long leash, trailed over his back and the terrace's paving stones.

His sniffing increased. He growled. His short nose swept across the slate-colored pavers. He retreated several steps as he tracked the scent, then followed it back to the grass. The clipped grass tickled his nose. He strained against the ribbon leash as he dug at the stones, as if the pavers were the edge of a cairn hiding a vicious rodent. Then his head popped up. Ears pricked forward. Dark eyes stared at the high hedge with its thick branches of boxwoods.

He glanced behind him at the woman holding one end of his tether. They had ended their walk by traversing the maze. Throughout their tour of the garden, she seemed distracted, barely attending to his tugs on the leash. Now her gaze focused on the drive that swept from the parkland. The gravel turned into a gentle curve as it approached the manor's forecourt. The little terrier sniffed the air. Then he lunged forward.

The leash held him back. He strained against it then lunged again, but his paws didn't find grass beneath him. His claws scrabbled on the pavers. He barked.

"No," the woman said and hauled back on the leash. "No, Sparky. We don't want another Incident with the Gardener."

Sparky whined. Incidents with the Gardener meant running and digging, shouts and a game of chase that left him lying on cool grass, panting to cool off, and being carried back to the house by his mistress.

Liza chuckled. "Come, Sparky."

He pranced back, his white patches gleaming against the brown and tan. She drew in the ribbon leash. When he pawed at her day gown, she picked him up and snuggled him close.

Sparky wiggled. He wanted down. He tolerated her snuggles, but he wanted to explore and dig and sniff out new adventures.

Liza felt the same way. Like Sparky, she often found herself restricted to the great manor, her activity confined to a Sparky-less stroll through the garden and maze, her curiosity limited to learning the people of Myers Montford and the village of Wellesbourne Montford. She had assumed none of the duties expected of the new wife of the lord of the manor. Her mother-in-law refused to cede even the pouring tea when the local families came to visit. After the business of her former life, Liza felt redundant.

Even the dinner parties hosted by the Myers offered her no enjoyment, for she barely knew their guests. And they watched her with avid eyes, eager to find mistakes by a commoner whose only grace was the wealth she brought into the marriage. Her adventures were staid rounds of visits to the sick and needy of the estate, monitored by her husband's sisters who reported to their mother, that great lady who refused to call herself *the dowager*.

Liza sighed into Sparky's coat. "I am bored," she whispered to the little terrier. He wiggled about, trying to give kisses then settled for licking her hand.

Liza stared again at the long drive with its neat edging.

When she'd come out with Sparky, a gardener had raked the gravel disturbed when her husband rode to the village. The gardener ignored her and continued his work until he removed the last trace of her husband Greville Myers' passage.

The whole estate was like that. Liza understood the need for everything in its place. Her own home, equal in size to the Myers Montford manor, had followed a strict routine and returned anything displaced immediately to its proper position. On her rounds carrying food and medicines to anyone sick or enfeebled, she saw well-tended fences, neat pastures and fields, all of which pleased her. The garden itself, allowed to decay at the fringes, had spent the summer months being restored.

Her husband had needed the marriage settlements she brought with her. He plowed the money back into the manor and estate. She had expected evidence of years of mismanagement, but only roofs and a few buildings needed obvious repairs. On the day she reached the estate, a month after their marriage, he hadn't appeared, leaving the greeting to his mother and sisters. He had no excuse, for Liza had announced her arrival with a note sent on the previous day. Instead, he chose to oversee repairs to a mucked-up irrigation weir. Liza understood the demands of an estate.

Yet his absence still hurt.

Without him there as the bridge, greeting his mother and sisters had quelled her spirit. Their stiff welcome was no more than any visitor would have received.

Six months married, and she still barely knew her husband. Five months in residence at the manor, and she still felt like a visitor. "How long will everyone stare at me, Sparky?" Were they waiting for the wealthy but decidedly middle-class bride to prove they should continue to look down their noses at her?

"When age or death or—or something else removes me from the estate, what then, Sparky? Will they rake out my passage just like that gardener? Will anyone ever know I lived here?"

The terrier wiggled and squirmed.

Liza set him down. He bit the leash, but the hastily tied ribbons withstood his sharp teeth.

"You would miss me, wouldn't you, Sparky?"

Busily biting a red ribbon, he ignored her, and Liza laughed at her silliness. She'd woken with a maudlin displacement. Something was wrong at Myers Montford. *Is that something me?*

To prevent another Incident with Mr. Potts the gardener, she had created the leash so she and Sparky could escape outside and thus avoid her in-laws. For two hours this afternoon she listened to Mrs. Myers describe in detail her plans for the upcoming fête to the sycophantic Victoria Pethbridge. The next hour she helped Cassandra select silks for a petit-point chair cover while Clarissa mulled over her watercolors. Liza desperately wanted this fresh air and sunshine.

Their walk successfully avoided another Incident with the Gardener, yet she couldn't bring herself to leave the terrace. Sparky tugged at the ribbons . "You need a proper leash. Tomorrow, I promise, we'll explore the gardens and the maze again."

His tail wagged at the promised treat.

Liza crossed her arms. Lifting her face to the warm sun, she closed her eyes and tried to drift like a tuft of dandelion. Her thoughts spun, though, like a maple seed, whirling round and round.

The distant crunch of horse hooves on gravel opened her eyes.

The rider lifted a hand. A wide-brimmed hat hid his features, but she recognized the horse, her husband's sorrel hunter, raw-boned but with a speed she envied.

Liza waved then wished she hadn't displayed so much enthusiasm. She felt his gaze until he disappeared, following the drive around the house to the stables.

Did Greville question their marriage as she did? Did he have regrets? She couldn't ask that. Except for his once-a-week visits to her chamber, they never met alone. They were husband and wife yet still strangers to each other.

Not for the first time she remembered the last Christmas party at her home in Sheffield. Gilbert Meaney had teased her with the suggestion that they elope. She had laughed and shaken her head. His apparent relief proved he wasn't serious. With her mother ensconced upstairs and her grandfather in London, he'd dared to kiss her, but he hadn't proposed again.

Then her grandfather returned, stuffed with pleasure because he'd found a husband for her, a gentleman who would elevate his own status. With a half-dozen mills churning out cloths and taxes for Britain, he wanted more to show for his efforts than coin. "No title but a blue-blood," he boasted. "As noble as they come."

She'd stared in horror as her fanciful dreams crashed around her.

Sparky whined then began barking. He strained at the leash. Nose to sky, he tugged at the leash then began hauling back, straining away from her.

"Sparky, what's wrong, boy? Whatever has disturbed you?"

Liza knelt, trying to soothe him, but he bounded to the length of his leash. He continued to strain, planting his feet and scrabbling at the pavers. The barking stopped, replaced by a low growl she'd never heard before.

"Sparky! No!"

He lunged. The leash caught him. Like a rampant lion on a shield, he pawed at the air.

Movement caught her eye. Liza stepped toward the little dog and towed on the leash, but she glanced at the glass doors that gave access to the side rooms.

A dark shape moved behind the glass panes. The sun's glare kept her from seeing more than shape.

The terrier gave a mighty lunge. The ribbon leash broke, and he plunged into the grass.

Liza sprang after him. She had to catch him before he dug up more of Mr. Potts' plants.

A crash shook the ground. Stone fragments peppered her.

She whirled around.

Rubble and dirt with bright red geraniums and their green petals lay scattered over the pavers. The remains of a urn had shattered on the terrace. The mass of dirt covered the stone slab where she'd stood.

Exactly where she'd stood.

Where it would have crushed her. She recognized the urn, one of the large decorative planters that adorned the low parapet surrounding the manor's roof. Mr. Potts and his boys had planted and nurtured the red cranesbill throughout the summer. "Six urns front and back, and six more each side," she could hear Mrs. Myers say. "Mr. Potts plants them to my specifications each year. This year we have the species *geranium*."

The world edged black.

Something whined and pressed against her leg.

Liza blinked.

Sparky whined and pawed at her skirt. She scooped him up and hugged him close. He had barked and fought the leash, trying to get her to move. Had he known the urn would fall? Had he seen it teetering?

"Smart dog! Oh, smart little dog. I love you!"

He wriggled and wanted to escape her arms.

Eyes still on the urn that would have killed her, Liza set him down but grabbed the much-shortened leash. The fall had destroyed the bright flowers and the urn's graceful shape. She looked up, but the bright sun blinded her.

How had the urn fallen?

Chapter 2

One of the glass-paned doors cracked open.

Liza still could not see who stood inside the door. Her eyes edged black again. The door shut. The shadowy shape moved away.

She stared at the destroyed urn. It would have killed her.

Sparky whined as he nosed the red geraniums.

I mustn't faint. The warning echoed through her mind. An eerie blackness replaced her whirling thoughts. She clutched at the leash, as if it were a life rope, like the stories she'd heard of sailors rescued from surf-broken ships.

Another terrace door opened.

"Mrs. Myers! Mrs. Myers! Ma'am, are you injured?"

The panicked voice broke her strange concentration. Liza jerked her eyes away from the rubble.

The butler Winston stood at the open door. He looked frozen with shock.

"Injured?" Even her voice sounded far away. The word had no meaning. Sparky still nosed the dirt. He pawed at a broken piece of the urn. "No. No," she repeated more sturdily. *Don't faint. Do not faint. If ever you thought you were strong, Liza girl, now's the time to prove it.* "Injured?" She looked down at herself. She didn't expect to see anything. She'd moved away before the urn landed. Yet as she smoothed her hand down her skirt, she saw a streak of red, brighter than the red ribbon she'd used as part of Sparky's leash.

"My word!" Winston disappeared into the house.

The red snared her eyes. She felt no pain. A curious numbness gripped her, spreading over her. She plucked the white skirt away from her body.

Winston returned. Servants crowded behind him. "Mrs. Myers, sit, please."

She needed to sit. She plopped onto the edge of a brick planter. That streak of red imprisoned her eyes.

"I have sent for the doctor, Mrs. Myers."

She stared at the butler then looked back at the blood. She still felt numb. She lifted a shaky hand—and saw blood on her fingers. She splayed her fingers, but they weren't injured.

Clarissa knelt before her. "She's bleeding. She's bleeding! What happened?"

Her gaze shifted to her sister-in-law. Clarissa had Greville's dark hair, his blue eyes, so deep, like a fathomless lake. For her, gender had softened the harder lines of his face and slimmed down his wide shoulders.

"Liza, you could have been killed."

"Yes" was all she could manage.

The leash was taken from her. Sparky growled as a servant dragged him away. He barked as he disappeared into the house.

"Sparky—."

"He is unharmed. You are bleeding. Winston, send for the doctor. And my brother rode to the village."

"Greville's back." Belatedly, she remembered the formal manners that this family maintained before their staff. "Mr. Myers just returned. He may be in the stable." Her voice came through a tunnel.

Clarissa rose. "Thank heavens. Winston—."

"I have sent for Doctor Chambers, Miss Myers."

"Find my brother."

"Yes, Miss Myers," but he didn't move. He had planted himself between Liza and the destruction. He issued orders to the footmen from that position.

Liza tried not to look, but her eyes kept focusing on the geraniums, the spray of five-petaled red flowers, scattered now, the green leaves crushed and releasing the distinctive fragrance, the crumbled blocks of hard stone that had once formed a graceful urn.

Clarissa picked up her hand. "Let's see what's causing this bleeding."

She saw it as her sister-in-law did, a single cut, just above her wrist. As if spotting it awoke the pain, the cut throbbed, a dull pulse increasing to a sharp ache.

Clarissa shook out a lacy handkerchief and pressed it to the cut. "You were lucky."

"Sparky pulled me away."

"He did? Good dog. He needs a treat for that. He's made up for the mess he made of my paintbrushes last week."

Winston stepped away. Liza looked up, hoping to see her husband only to be confronted with her mother-in-law's scowl.

Amabel Coughran Myers, a widow for several years, had deigned to walk to the terrace. From the beginning Liza had admired the woman's pale beauty, gold and creamy and pale blue, with the slenderness of strict discipline and the height of a Nordic warrior maiden. She had certainly engaged her daughter-in-law in a fierce albeit subtle battle. Now, with her golden hair gleaming in the sunlight, she looked like a Valkyrie come to claim her portion of the dead from the battlefield. "She is hurt?"

"Something must have struck her, Mama. One of the urns fell."

Mrs. Myers didn't look at the roof. "Is that her only injury?"

With effort, Liza clawed her wits out of the corners they had scurried into. Never would she cede the field. "It is only a minor scratch, ma'am."

"Has the doctor been sent for? Winston?"

The butler turned from speaking to a maid. The young woman scurried away. "Yes, ma'am. I did so immediately."

"That is unnecessary." Liza struggled to her feet, fighting Clarissa's attempt to keep her seated. "I am not injured. This is not even deep." She took the handkerchief away from Clarissa and pressed the cut hard to staunch the blood. "We need to clear this mess away." Energy shook her as an inner reserve poured out more strength. "We should send for Mr. Potts. He should inspect the other urns, to ensure that another one will not crash onto someone less fortunate. Winston, will you see to that?"

"Yes, Mrs. Myers."

She stepped forward, and the remaining servants eddied back. "Has my husband been told?"

"I am not certain, ma'am."

"What is she suggesting?" Amabel Myers turned to her oldest daughter. "Surely she doesn't think—."

Cassandra Myers burst onto the terrace. "Heavens! What happened here? Victoria, come and see."

At that name, Liza clutched every wit and strength remaining to her so she would not fail against the young woman her husband had once favored with his attentions.

The Myers women were pretty, which cast her own nondescript features into plainness. Her handsome husband with his strong features and lake-deep eyes had taken Liza's breath when first she'd met him. She still wasn't quite adept at concealing the effect one of his focused looks had on her.

Eight years older and master of Myers Montford since his father's death, he had never claimed a puritanical life. She knew the estate's dire need of funds had forced him into the despised role of a fortune hunter. She wished, fiercely and desperately with every passing day, that Greville had informed her of one salient point—that he'd thrown over a diamond of the first water as his fiancée in order to rescue his manor and estate.

Victoria Pethbridge was that diamond of the first water. She had the accepted beauty of dark hair and startling green eyes, high cheekbones and a creamy complexion, and a swan's neck that formed the perfect setting for the simple cameo she always wore. She moved with a swan's grace as well, never hurried, never ruffled. At their first meeting, Liza's envy had reared its ugly head. By their second meeting, she knew of Victoria's almost-engagement to Greville. Minutes before Victoria entered the house, the dowager had informed Liza. Then those cold blue eyes watched every detail of Liza's reaction to the news and their second meeting.

As vicar's daughter, Victoria was well-liked and welcomed in every household of the parish. While other people became flurried and flustered, her serenity remained intact.

Now she glided onto the terrace. The sea of servants parted for her, giving her a straight path to Liza. She glanced at the rubble as she passed it. Dark as her hair, her winged brows lifted. She looked from the broken cast-stone to Liza, still clutching Clarissa's lacy handkerchief, now ruined by blood. Victoria's green eyes narrowed as she crossed the remaining feet.

"What a fortunate escape. That urn is quite ruined. The flowers cannot be recovered, I believe. You have only that injury? You sustained nothing else?"

Like Mrs. Myers, she never used Liza's name, neither her Christian name nor her married one. The rush of energy that had infused Liza began draining away. No one but she had ever remarked on Victoria's refusal to say her name. Once Liza noticed it, she could not help marking it on every occasion. It was a small insult, as subtle as Mrs. Myers' insult.

The Latins used to say *Still waters run deep*. Did Victoria bear a grudge against Liza? She wore a cheerful mask, but the occasional flash of anger shot from those green eyes, surprising enmity from a vicar's daughter. Had Victoria been on the roof? That comment about the falling urn had sounded *off*.

Will God forgive me for thinking Victoria had anything to do with the urn falling?

"Only this," and she lifted her arm to answer Victoria's question, "which is nothing. I have indeed had a fortunate *escape*."

Those green eyes narrowed. Victoria hadn't missed Liza's emphasis. "How did it miss you?"

"Sparky pulled me away."

"That dog! Where is he?"

"He's been taken to Mrs. Myers' chamber, Miss Pethbridge."

"What brings you to us today, Victoria?" Liza heard the hard edge in her question. One part of her was appalled at that sharp question. Another part wished that Victoria would stay home for a solid week.

The young woman found an excuse to visit the manor every other day. Ostensibly she came to help with the planning of the fête, but she always managed to plant herself near Greville.

Mrs. Myers scowled, a fierce fighter for her protégée. "You know that Victoria must come every day this week and the next to write invitations for the fête. She is so kind to offer her assistance to me. I cannot depend on anyone else."

"Perhaps we should not work on the invitations today, Mrs. Myers." Victoria's modulated words fell smoothly into the silence after her mentor's defense. "With this upset today, should we delay the festival?"

"I am not upset," Liza demurred, but the sisters' clamor against any delay drowned her out.

"Not have the fête? We must have the fête," Cassandra cried. "Everyone looks forward to it. You can't cancel it, Mama. Promise me that you will not do that."

"The fête is three weeks away," Clarissa pointed out. "Liza will have more than enough time to recover from any upset. Besides, we must hold the festival this year. For three years, Greville has forced us to cancel it. Everyone is eagerly anticipating this year."

The things I learn when people don't heed me. As the girls confronted their mother and Victoria, Liza considered what she'd just learned. No one had mentioned the previous cancellations. *Cancelled because Greville forced them.* No wonder his sisters were so excited about planning the festival. As the villagers would be equally excited.

Like the repairs to the house and the estate, her money doubtless funded the festival's return.

Avoiding the debris, she edged toward Winston. The butler was ordering the remaining servants back to their work.

Her knees felt shakier than before. She'd never panicked in her life, but Victoria's *How did it miss you?* had sapped the last of her energy. She wanted to retreat to her room and cry into Sparky's coat.

The world dimmed, as if a cloud passed over the sun on this cloudless day. She blinked, losing the glass-paned door in the sudden dimness.

Height and broad shoulders blocked her stumbling flight.

Liza looked up, into her husband's scowl. His hands clamped onto her shoulders. "What has happened here? Are you hurt?"

A sob broke out. Then the light dimmed entirely, and she sank under the weight of Greville's hands.

Chapter 3

Greville caught Elizabeth as she dropped. He scooped her up. In his arms she seemed surprisingly slim and fragile. Out of his arms she was like a mysterious elemental force, one that he wanted to grasp and understand. The difference shocked him.

Thick lashes concealed her eyes, a rich brown with elusive glints of amber, distracting him whenever he delved deeply into conversation with her. Her cheeks had lost all color. Whatever had occurred had overset her determined personality. He saw no tear-streaks, but he would not expect those. His wife never cried. She would shrink from his mother's acidity and wince at Cassandra's unthinking comments. She had uprooted her life and come to his home, yet she still wafted like a dandelion tuft, seeking a planting ground, drifting with the vagaries of her new life.

Yet now she swooned, another unexpected reaction.

He studied the debris on the terrace then judged the distance it had fallen from the parapet. How close had the urn come to striking her? Crushing her? Killing her?

"Allow me, sir." Winston flourished a large handkerchief. He folded it then pressed it to Elizabeth's arm. After tying it deftly, he stepped aside.

"She's hurt?"

"A scratch only." Clarissa came closer. She tucked Elizabeth's dangling arm across her slender body. She glanced down, and Greville followed her gaze. A froth of lace lay on a paving stone. Blood stained it.

"Sir, if you will bring the young Mrs. Myers this way." Winston opened a glass-paned door farther along the terrace.

"Open the door to my study," he ordered.

The butler froze only a second at the unusual order, then he sprang to obey. Greville's study was sacrosanct territory that not even his mother entered. He had a moment to worry about any precedent he might set, but the Elizabeth he had come to know during their brief weeks of marriage would never intrude.

As he followed Winston, Greville noticed that his mother had disappeared, likely returning to her sitting room where she delegated her duties to others. Cassandra used a toe to poke at pieces of the rubble.

Victoria Pethbridge caught his eyes. Her mouth twitched, a habit when she forced herself to keep silent. Turning, she called to his younger sister. "Come, Cassandra, we have invitations to write. It looks as if Clarissa is abandoning us."

"Do go on," Clarissa urged from behind him. "I think Elizabeth is recovering."

His wife had stirred, and he hadn't noticed. He carried her through the second glass-paned door that Winston held open. He hesitated only a second then lowered his fragile burden to the old sofa with its sagging cushions. Then he knelt beside her and watched the flicker of her thick eyelashes, proof that Clarissa was right. The swoon was only temporary.

Elizabeth's hair had loosened from its severe bun at her nape. Long and wavy, it trailed over his arm as he shifted her head to a cushion. By day she wore it in a bun or a braided coronet. At night she confined it in a long plait. A brown lock had separated from the mass. He slipped his fingers along the silken tress, an untangled skein of common color that was beautiful in a subtle way.

Just like her eyes, unnoticed until he had looked closely.

Another distraction when he needed to concentrate around her.

Those amber-flecked eyes opened. Elizabeth blinked then struggled to sit upright.

Greville pressed her down. "You've had a shock, Elizabeth."

Her eyes widened. Her color receded even more. Then those dark lashes dropped. "I wish you called me 'Liza'," she murmured. Belatedly hearing her words, her eyes shot open, wide and alarmed. Once more she struggled to sit.

"Liza, lie still." *Why didn't she ask that before?* Six months married, and he still used her full name, not the shortened familiar. *Liza*. Six months. And today was the third, the day of their marriage last April.

A pretty color pinked her cheeks. She subsided again and resolutely shut her eyes. "I'm not a feeble invalid."

Behind him, Clarissa giggled. "Certainly not, Elizabeth. Liza," she amended. "I have a drink for you. Move, Brother." She crowded in, holding a glass of amber liquid. She had raided his whiskey decanter. '

Elizabeth—Liza, he must remember—lifted up to sip the liquid. She swallowed then coughed and gasped and waved another sip away. "Thank you." She finished sitting up, but Clarissa's perch on the sofa prevented her from swinging her lower limbs to the floor. "I should like to retire to my chamber."

Greville winced. "I should like for you to stay here until the doctor has attended you."

Her lashes lifted. She gave him a direct look. Too quickly, though, her gaze faltered and dropped to her lap. "Dr. Chambers is surely delivering the Holdstock baby, over at the mill."

The mill was beyond the estate's park, on the road to the village. He folded his arms. "We will wait for his arrival."

"I wasn't injured."

"We will wait together, Liza."

Her receded blush returned. She looked at her hands, twisting in her lap. He watched, counting the rapid rise and fall of her breasts. Had she blushed this second time at his use of her preferred name or because he said they would wait together?

That was not a question he dared to ask, however much he wanted the answer. As Clarissa protested that Elizabeth's injury required a doctor's attention, Greville puzzled over the reason he had never called her *Liza*. He remembered his visits to her home in Sheffield, first in January to meet his prospective bride then in April to marry her. Her mother and her grandfather had called her *Liza*. When he arrived at her home in April, the wedding ceremony mere hours away, he had limited himself to *Miss Corbett*.

On his arrival, as a footman led Greville to her grandfather's study, Liza had intercepted him. "I would have things clear between us, Mr. Myers. "Brown eyes wide, she had asked, "We are going to marry, then? Marry after only a few days of acquaintance?"

The question stung. On his visit in January he had signed the betrothal papers, but he hadn't attempted to become acquainted with the plain woman he planned to marry. Hating the position debt forced him into, his "of course" came out brusque, like chipped stone. She had winced, and he berated himself. Yet he needed to marry her. He'd already signed the contract to replace the manor's slate roof. Then would come the repairs to the attics and the chimneys. Restoration to other estate buildings would follow—the stables, the dairy barn, the piggery, the hay barn, grain silos. Without making a list, he already had a dozen uses for the money she brought into the marriage.

Elizabeth had arrived at Myers Montford in May, a full month after their marriage. She hadn't traveled with him, pleading a need to pack her necessary possessions. Torrential spring rains lengthened her delay. Those same rains had flooded the pond and caused the weir to collapse. Winston sent a runner to inform him of her arrival, but he didn't return to the manor until sunset, needing every bit of the light to repair the dam.

Greville had delayed the weir's repair for weeks. Other essential repairs had crowded before it. He paid for that delay by not meeting his wife on her arrival to his home. No matter what he said, his family misconstrued his non-attendance when Elizabeth arrived. The servants had likely reached similar conclusions. And those conclusions—wrong though they were—had spread far into the community.

He had expected Elizabeth's censure. She mutely shouldered the offense—and delayed taking up the reins that his mother should have ceded to her.

Now, a small brown sprite on the sagging sofa, Liza looked up. Her gaze searched his before skittering away. Only then did Greville feel the heavy lines creasing his brow.

"I don't know how that urn could have fallen," Clarissa exclaimed, filling the silence between husband and wife. "I was on the parapet only yesterday. I noticed no problems."

His wife cleared her throat. "You go up to the roof walk?"

"Almost daily. The parapet goes all the way around. Did Mama not tell you of it when she showed you the house?"

"Our mother wouldn't consider the parapet," Greville reminded his sister. He kept his voice soft so he wouldn't discompose Eliza—Liza. "She hates the narrow stairs that lead to the box room. That's the access to the roof."

"That is true," Clarissa admitted. "Mama has funny dislikes. You must come up with me, Elizabeth. The view is stupendous. Come tomorrow. You can see over the fields and the park, and from the west you can see the bell tower of the village church."

Liza said nothing. "I think not tomorrow," Greville said for her, as the study door opened to admit the butler, "not for a few days. Winston, we should have Potts examine the other urns."

"Mrs. Myers has requested that, sir. The young Mrs. Myers," he clarified.

"I wouldn't have had the sense to think of that," Clarissa marveled, and Greville recognized another facet of his unknown wife. A few days to meet her, another handful to marry her, and five months since her arrival. In all that time, they'd spent very little of it in actual conversation.

"Mr. Winston," a woman's voice said, and the butler turned to speak with the maid. Over Winston's shoulder Greville saw the middle-aged woman who attended his wife. Mercy had traveled with Liza from Sheffield, and she had no hesitation to ensure the best care for her mistress. "Beggin' pardon, sir," she was telling Winston, "but I've good strong tea for Mrs. Myers."

Winston began to send her away, but Greville interrupted. "Let her enter."

Carrying a flowered china tea set, the maid trod across the Persian carpet as if it were no different than the planked flooring. She placed the silver tray on a little table then drew it closer to the sofa before she poured cream in a cup, added liberal spoons of sugar, then poured in the tea. She stirred rapidly, tapped the spoon to the saucer three times then handed the tea to her mistress. "There. Drink all of that now. There's nothing that a good strong cuppa won't set to rights."

Liza paused with the teacup at her lips. "You know that's not true, Mercy."

The maid flashed a look at Greville. She folded her hands over her stomach. "Aye, miss, but tea sets it going toward right, that you have to admit."

His wife gave a little nod. Then she blew across the steaming liquid and took a cautious sip. The maid gave a nod. She produced a ribbon and tied back Liza's hair into a school-girl's pony tail. Then she curtsied and retreated.

Clarissa rose with the grace her mother had instilled in her three children. "Elizabeth looks much better, doesn't she, Greville? Not so pale."

"Liza does," he agreed, firmly saying her name.

His sister gave a single nod then followed his reminder. "Shall I stay, Liza? Until the doctor comes. And even then?"

She lowered the floral cup with its yellow buttercup and gilded edge. Her brown eyes were wide and serious in her blanched face. "I am not hurt, Clarissa. It is just a deep scratch. Although I do believe your handkerchief is ruined."

"Tut, what's a hankie. I will stay if you wish, Liza."

Her lips curved in a tiny smile, and with surprise Greville realized he'd seen that subtle smile a few times—when she watched her little terrier, when Potts directed the flowers from the garden to her, and when she mastered a particularly difficult piece without missing a note of the music. Last Sunday, he remembered, when the vicar and his family came to dine and Cook served an apple delight instead of the ice cream his mother had ordered. That was the last time he'd seen that smile.

On the Monday after that dinner, he sat down to a painful luncheon. His mother demanded that he reprimand the cook for changing her menu. Before he sent for Mrs. Timmons, Liza intercepted him on his way to the study. With a frowning concern for Cook, she asked to take the blame for the change of dessert, for no ice had remained for the vicar's favorite sweet.

Now Clarissa's concern won that subtle smile. "I am not hurt," his wife repeated, "just shocked."

"I would have screamed *murder* if that urn had nearly fallen on me."

"You are overly dramatic, Rissa."

She gave a cheery agreement with her brother's statement then chided, "But you have no feelings, Grev. The size of that urn, the weight as it crashed down. Where were you that you didn't hear that boom? It shook the windows all along the terrace."

"I was delayed leaving the stable."

She snorted inelegantly, and Liza's smile widened. "You're delaying, Clarissa, when I know that your mother particularly requested you speak with Mrs. Timmons about the menus for the weekend."

"A task you should be doing. I do not know why Mama refuses to turn it over to you. She complains every time Cook makes a change. She completely ignores the fact that she is at fault for refusing to listen when Cook speaks up." She sailed from the room, the study door held open by the butler, and left an awkward silence in her wake.

"Sir, I should check on Potts."

"Do that, Winston," Greville agreed.

The butler shut the door, leaving Greville and his wife alone.

Chapter 4

Liza focused on her teacup. Greville retreated to his desk. He didn't want to loom over her.

In January, on his visit to the Corbett home, her grandfather had towered over her as he dictated some order to her. Seated in one of the over-stuffed chairs that the old man preferred, Liza looked cowed while Corbett shook a finger over her bent head. Greville didn't know what the tirade had covered. Corbett had broken off when he entered. Within a few minutes he shared that his granddaughter was amenable to a marriage proposal from a gentleman like Greville Myers of Myers Montford, an old name, long established and connected to a duke.

She had said nothing. She hadn't nodded or shaken her head, only looked at her clasped hands.

With the prospects of marriage settlements to relieve his financial issues, Greville hadn't questioned her lack of response.

His wife was determined; that he knew. On her arrival, she demanded a place be found for her spinet, brought with her in a freight wagon behind her carriage. She insisted that her brown-and-white terrier be allowed access to more than her chambers. She wanted him to have the run of the public rooms in the house. She stood up to Potts when he complained the little dog was a menace to the flowers.

Yet he'd seen her close off, as she had with her grandfather, when his mother rebuffed Liza's interest in the household and when Victoria claimed no assistance for the Midsummer Parish Bazaar was needed. Victoria had then enlisted his sisters' help. His mother complained constantly about dealing with servants and wanted Clarissa to plan the meals, bypassing his wife yet again.

If he ordered the changes, they would happen.

He waited for Liza to look up. When she delayed, he sighed loudly.

Her gaze flashed up then returned to her teacup, empty now except for a last sip with bits of tea leaves.

He needed to break the silence between them. "That tea has cooled. Shall I ring for another pot?"

She bestowed herself, straightening her spine and shoulders, transferring her gaze to the teapot strewn with flowers and gilt paint. Then she returned the cup and saucer to the tray. "That is not necessary." She lifted her chin. Her gaze held a glint of—was that humor? "Mercy's idea of strong tea is not mine. She adds medicinal herbs."

Ah. To keep her talking and with no idea what to say, he tried, "I don't recognize that pattern of tea service." When she winced, he knew that he'd stuck another spanner in the works.

"It is my own tea service. Mercy unpacked a single set for my personal use. The rest remains crated in the box room."

"I see. Would you like to use it every day?"

His mother favored a garish tobacco leaf pattern and the ornate silver serving set from his grandmother's day, when the estate had spent more money on appearances than the necessities. Last week, bidden to take tea at his mother's command, he'd noticed the china had chips and cracks. For an awkward half-hour he sat beside Victoria, the woman he'd once thought to marry, while his wife was consigned to a chair barely within the circle. Concentrating on the estate's recovery, he had let such slights slip past him. Victoria wanted to talk. He filled her ears with the lame plow horse, the dray that had lost a wheel, and the estate' best harvest in years before he escaped when the clock struck the full hour.

"I do use my tea service daily," Liza was responding. "Mercy uses it for my morning tea."

"No, I mean—." *What do I mean?* "Does it have enough settings for a dozen people?"

"It's a service for twenty-four." Her brow had furrowed, as if she didn't know why he would ask about a tea service.

He didn't know either, but he persisted, keen to atone for months of slights. "Would you be willing to use it as the house tea service?"

Her brow cleared. That mask shuttered down, hiding all emotions. "You intend that my tea service replace the chinoiserie service currently in use?"

"Yes."

"Your mother was not inclined—."

"My mother is not the lady of the house."

Her mouth fell open. She shut it with a click of teeth. "I do not intend to displace your mother."

"I intend it," he declared, "but shall we make the changes gradual? Clarissa obviously does not enjoy planning the meals, and my mother obviously no longer cares to do it. She should have ceded that responsibility to you, as the new lady of the house."

"I did mention—."

She so obviously bit her tongue that he had a hard time not chuckling. He decided to solve another problem. "My mother also does not enjoy dealing with the daily household minutiae that Mrs. Grunby brings to her attention. Are you willing to shoulder that burden?" Liza nodded even as he had a horrid thought, a lack that would be a true affront to his wife. "Did Mrs. Grunby give you a tour of the house and the staff when you arrived?"

Color rushed to her cheeks, giving him the answer. All she said was "an abbreviated tour."

So. He'd learned two more things about his wife—she wouldn't complain and she created circumstances that she wanted within the prescribed cage others put her in, as she had with her spinet and her pet and her personal tea service. He had no difficulty believing she'd learned those traits while living with her overbearing grandfather.

Adam Corbett's house, which he fancifully called Corbett Towers, was larger than Myers Montford. He had purchased it from a childless marquess desperate to escape punishing debt. Liza's mother had claimed to manage it, but he'd seen the servants seek out the daughter when problems arose. Luxury enveloped him during his two stays, from the appointments in his room to the fare at table.

The subtle wealth of the house contrasted with the old man himself. Corbett had worn flamboyant red and orange when he accosted Greville at his club in London. In April, when he was forced on a tour of Corbett Towers, he discovered the Sheffield house lacked only Montford's sprawling lands. Corbett had queried the manor's number of rooms and chimneys and windows before he rested his hands on his round belly, well satisfied that his house was larger. He frowned at Greville's monochromatic attire and flashed rings on both hands. "Cor, you're plain as a parson," he'd remarked on the wedding day. "My Liza is somber as you."

He hadn't believed the man, not even when his bride walked the altar in simple pastels. Looking back on the past months, though, he realized Liza wore less jewelry and fewer vivid colors than his mother did. Her only experiment with flamboyance came at the Midsummer Ball, when she wore a crimson gown trimmed with black ribbons and froths of white lace. The stark contrast gave her an unexpected prettiness that had opened his eyes.

A sharp two-rap knock fell on the study door, Winston's usual signal. "Come," Greville called, eager to implement changes that were five months delayed.

The butler opened the door wide. "Sir. Mr. Potts wishes to speak with you."

"And I wish to speak with him. No, Liza," he added, for she had stood as if she would retreat. "I wish you to remain." He waited until she subsided on the sofa, her hand clutching the rounded arm as if she needed to steady herself. "Winston, please inform Mrs. Grunby and Mrs. Timmons that they should report directly to my wife and no longer to my mother. Or my sisters."

He didn't mistake the butler's gleam. His wife had an ally in the man. How many others had she won over by not pushing into her rightful position? Clever Liza.

"Sir, does that also mean that Miss Pethbridge will no longer issue orders?"

"Good Lord! Has the vicar's daughter been ordering my household?"

He'd thought Victoria's constant visits to the manor were based on friendship with his sisters and the occasional help to his mother. How many duties had his mother turned over to Victoria in anticipation of his marriage to her? She should have stopped requiring Victoria's help last winter, when he returned from Sheffield and announced his plans to marry an heiress to recover their fortunes. Since his mother continued to enlist Victoria's unnecessary help and refused to cede the chatelaine responsibilities to the new lady of the house, his mother had obviously thrown her own version of a tantrum against his marriage.

Eyes on Liza, he added, "That includes Miss Pethbridge, Winston. She should no longer dip a finger into my household." His wife's pinked cheeks rewarded him.

"Excellent, sir." The butler's response reinforced Winston's alliance to Liza. "Mr. Potts, sir." He waited until the head gardener entered then shut the door with a decided click of the lock.

In the last decade, while the gardens shrank and dozens of staff were released, Potts had remained. Working alone, the man had slaved to keep the kitchen garden and the rose garden and the estate hedges intact. Everything else grew rampant. In the last six months, his staff restored, the head gardener gave first attention to the maze, a centerpiece from the days of Queen Elizabeth. From a simple knot garden, the maze had grown into high boxwood hedges that hid its secret unless walkers had the key.

Potts didn't give his loyalty cheaply. Before Greville's marriage, he had flowers brought to the house and left in the stillroom. With Liza's advent, the old gardener sent flowers daily, to the stillroom and to her private chambers, proof of his choice for lady of the house.

Twisting his battered felt hat, the man stopped before Greville's desk but turned so that he didn't give his back to Liza. His mother would have sniffed at Potts' stained trousers and frayed knitted vest. A lanky giant, he towered over Greville. "Mrs. Myers, ma'am, 'tis sorry I am that the great urn nearly struck you down. Never reckoned it would fall, that I didn't. Might have killed you, ma'am."

She stood. For a second, she hesitated, then she stepped to Greville's side. He tucked her fairy fingers in the crook of his arm and let her speak.

"Mr. Potts, I requested that you inspect the other urns, to ensure they are in no danger of toppling over."

"I been up and done that, ma'am. Not a one is about to fall. It were a quick check, mind, but I'll go again soon as I leave here."

"I wish to go with you, Potts." Greville inserted. "I want to inspect how the urn fell from its pediment."

The weather-roughed gardener scratched his thin hair. "That puzzles me, sir, a right puzzle. I always plant the urns m'self. The boys do the watering. Coming on the end of the season, I went up a couple of weeks ago and looked over them *geranium*. I didn't see no sign of trouble with the urns then."

Potts' statement tallied with Clarissa's, but "We will inspect them together."

The gardener bobbed his head. "Aye, sir. Ma'am. A couple of m'boys are clearing away what's left of that urn. I'm glad that you weren't hurt."

"Just a scratch, Potts." She lifted her arm, displaying Winston's handkerchief and the streak of dried blood tracking down to her hand.

His hat twisted around again. "Somebody said that your little dog saved you."

"Yes. He broke the ribbons that I had tied into a leash. If I hadn't started after Sparky—." She swayed. Greville stepped closer, supporting her with his body. Her hand tightened on his arm, and she leaned into his frame. "Sparky saved me," she whispered.

"Aye, ma'am. I won't be calling that little dog what I called him." He cleared his throat. Digging into his pocket, he fished out a tight coil of leather cord, braided to form a loop on one end. He placed it on the desk. "For the dog, ma'am. I reckon he needs more than ribbons for his leash."

Liza picked up the coil. The loop earned special attention. "How clever. His collar will fit into this. Thank you, Mr. Potts. This is an ideal replacement for the ribbons. Sparky was chewing through them."

Red tinted the gardener's freckled face. "Aye, ma'am. Sir. Should I wait for you at the little stair?"

"Do that, please."

As soon as the gardener turned away, Liza walked over to the windows.

Greville remembered how she had come to his side to present a united front to Potts. Then she had leaned into his support. The fallen urn had shaken his complacency.

What had that urn broken in his wife? That sturdy barrier she kept rebuilding around herself. This time, he refused to let her repair it.

Arms folded, with the coiled leash dangling from one hand, Liza stared at the terrace.

"You made a leash for your dog out of ribbons?" Question out, he mentally kicked himself. Of a thousand ways to win his wife, he'd chosen the worst.

She glanced over her shoulder. Her pony-tail slipped across her shoulders, a silken rope that lured him near. "I had nothing else to use as a leash. The ribbons were a solution. Sparky was desperate to go outside. So was I. They have served since May."

A third exhibit of his wife's determination not to let circumstances cage her.

He joined her at the window. A youth picked up the broken pieces of the urn. Another shoveled up the dirt with the crushed cranesbills. The debris filled a wheelbarrow.

"I believe it may be time to remove all of the urns," he ventured then waited.

"That's—." She stopped. He nearly spoke twice before she started again. "That is not necessary. I would not wish the architecture of the house to change."

"My grandfather added them. If I am to choose between the appearance of my house or my wife's safety, then I will choose her safety."

The scrawny boy, all elbows and knees, began sweeping the dirt while the other picked up the smaller bits of cast-stone. Red petals flew before the clods of dirt and landed on the grass.

"You will not need to remove them all. Perhaps you could leave the ones at the corners."

"I will have all of them removed, Liza. You will never look at this house and think only luck saved your life."

"Luck and Sparky." Then she gasped.

Greville leaned forward to see.

The broom had cleared away the covering dirt. Where the urn had struck, the paving stones were shattered.

Chapter 5

Greville wrapped an arm around his wife's shoulders, his forearm inches above her pounding heart. He pressed a kiss to the silky crown of her head. "Never again," he vowed. "You need not worry about those urns ever again, Liza."

At his use of her name, Liza's heart gave a little skip then resumed its rapid beat. Fearing she would betray herself, she stirred, planning to step away from him. "Potts is waiting for you."

"Damn Potts," he muttered.

He turned her about. Those lake-deep eyes bored into hers. Liza wanted to hide from their scrutiny, but she would not shut out her newly considerate husband. "I must meet with the housekeeper and the cook."

"Damn them, too," but he smiled.

The heavy weight of his hands did not feel like a cage. They reassured, like a heavy cloak on an icy day. Comfort rather than oppression. "I thank you for giving those responsibilities to me. It will be more like home." When his dark brows came down, she regretted the words. She intended no recriminations. The days weighed heavier than his hands when she had so little to do.

"I remember how well you managed your grandfather's house, which you had doubtless done from the time you and your mother went to live with him."

His words seemed to hold a question, but her pounding heart and his heavy hands had combined to shorten her breath. She backtracked into safety. "I will enjoy talking with your cook about the meals. She is an artist in the kitchen."

His hands fell away, and her contrary soul missed their weight. She slipped around him, ensuring her escape before Greville realized that he'd stolen her heart weeks and weeks ago.

"You are certain that you are well enough?"

She lifted her arm. "Truly, it is only a scratch."

Winston knocked then admitted a dark-suited man with military whiskers.

Flushed from his haste, Dr. Chambers hustled in, a black valise preceding him. "You have an injury, Mrs. Myers?"

Liza turned to the doctor with relief. "The merest scratch, I assure you."

"You will let me judge that, young lady." He plunked his medical bag on Greville's desk, as if he had a right to take over the space. "Your butler tells me that you were nearly killed."

The doctor had sunken eyes with deep pouches, a sign of the dissipation to which some military men were prone. She disliked his brusque manner, but in her few months at Montford, she'd seen his obvious care for his patients and his love of his three boys. After her first month here, she had finally consulted him, an awkward conversation of half-statements and wishes. Those eyes, so like a basset hound, had stared fixedly before he cleared his throat and gave strict instructions that she found sensible.

Liza resumed her seat on the sagging sofa and lifted her arm, still bandaged with a man's handkerchief. She didn't remember when that had happened nor who had sacrificed that square of linen to staunch the bloodflow.

Greville positioned himself at her right hand as the doctor untied the handkerchief. "Winston did not exaggerate, Chambers. A roof urn nearly struck her when it fell."

"One of those great pots with the red flowers?" Dragging over a chair, he perched on its hard edge to examine the revealed scratch. "May I?" he murmured but didn't wait for consent. He gripped her forearm and angled it to the sunlight. "This is not deep, luckily."

"It bled a lot," Greville offered.

"A little blood looks like a lot." He released her arm, and she rested it in her lap while he talked of salves and new bandages three times a day. "You may have a bruise pop out." He rummaged in his bag then returned with a compress and a salve.

Hoping to distract him, she asked, "Did Mrs. Holdstock have her baby?"

"Twins. Easy as pie. This is her third lie-in. First birth is the hardest. Any signs of that?"

Why did the doctor never consider her privacy? "No."

"Still regular? No more pain? Do you use the salve I gave you?"

Her face burned. Her husband's gaze had sharpened, and he scrutinized her more closely than he ever had. "Yes, my courses remain regular," she hastily answered. "Yes to the salve. No more pain."

Chambers nodded. His focus remained on applying the salved compress to her arm then winding a cloth around it. He tied the bandage then clapped his hands to his knees. "There, that's that, then. Should that scratch become tender and sore past the second day, you send for me immediately."

"She fainted," Greville inserted, preventing her escape from the doctor.

"What's that?" Those sunken eyes narrowed.

"My wife fainted. Afterward."

"Not immediately," she protested. She had to endure a closer inspection of her eyes, a check of her pulse, and a listen to her heart.

"Not hit in the head? Or anywhere else?"

"No. I am not a fool, Dr. Chambers. I would tell you."

Greville loomed over them, much as her grandfather did when he wanted to enforce his will. She disliked it, so she kept her attention on the doctor.

"I would hope that you would inform me, Mrs. Myers, but I find you a little too reticent." He stood up, not a short man, but he still had to look up at her tall husband. "Delayed shock. I've seen it. Soldiers conking out after their first battle. She's not truly hurt. She's fit."

"Just as I said," but the doctor ignored her insertion.

"Heartbeat's good. Got her wits. Myself, I might be screaming with terror. I know the size of those pots." He closed his medical bag. "Anyone else here got any hurts?" Those hound eyes narrowed even more. "Maybe to their hands?"

"I thought of that," Greville said while Liza wondered what Dr. Chambers meant. "Nothing has been brought to my attention. I will mention it, however, to several people."

"See that you do. I'll take my leave then. Got a broken leg to check over at the Davenports. Good day to you, Mrs. Myers, Mr. Myers." He was gone as rapidly as he'd come.

Her husband waited for the door to close before he asked, "Dr. Chambers gave you a salve for pain?" With his arms across his broad chest, he loomed even more than usual and clearly expected an answer. "Are you not well?"

Those last words gave her an opportunity to retort, "I am in excellent health. Dr. Chambers said so." She jumped to her feet.

Greville snared her wrist and stopped her escape. "What is the salve for, Liza?"

At the gentle question, her face flamed, a telltale sign that she wished she'd left behind with her girlhood. Even Gilbert Meaney had teased her about her flushes. "When—when—." She couldn't express it. She didn't have the words.

"When I come to your chamber?"

His rumble reminded her of his brief comments when he joined with her. Refusing to bear his closer scrutiny, Liza stared at the long fingers encircling her wrist. His skin was so much darker than her own. His mother had complained about his tan. He'd shrugged off her scold with a single comment about working in the fields. She like the tan, a sign that he wasn't a hoity-toity gentleman too refined to dirty his hands with honest work.

"I had thought—." He sighed, also unable to discuss their intimate moments. "My apologies. My intentions for you are not pain."

Her lashes flew up. She swallowed as she met his blue eyes. His frown wasn't for her but reflective of his dissatisfaction—no, anger—at himself. "It is not as it was. I assure you."

His "thank God" was heartfelt. He lifted her hand and traced his fingers over the doctor's bandage. "We've changes ahead of us, Liza."

Suspecting he meant more than those she knew, she still nodded agreement.

He parted from her at the stairs, for the butler stood there, clearly lurking to intercept her.

Liza watched Greville bound up the steps. The falling urn had focused her husband's attention on her. Liza found herself fiercely glad of the event.

"Ma'am," Winston said.

She towed her gaze from her disappearing husband.

"Mrs. Grunby and the cook are eager to meet with you, ma'am. I thought the smaller sitting room."

The larger sitting room was her mother-in-law's domain. The butler clearly did not want to challenge more of the status quo. Yet Greville's decision to grant her these responsibilities might spark a fire for change. No one, however, wanted a blazing conflagration.

"May I visit them in their offices?"

"Mrs. Grunby is in her office now, ma'am. While you meet with her, I can inform Mrs. Timmons."

"We have our solution, Winston."

The dour butler allowed a small smile to grace his rigidly controlled expression.

Behind a green baize door that marked the staff's domain lay a descending stair that bent back on itself. On her previous tour, Liza hadn't seen Belowstairs. She eagerly looked around, trying to get a feel for the working of staff.

A long hall ran through the center of the house, stretching from one end to another, with high windows to admit natural light. Rooms opened to each side, with doors opened to reveal their various purposes. Clad in a dark grey livery, servants bustled in and out, like bees at a hive, performing tasks that kept great houses running smoothly. At her grandfather's house, Liza had regularly visited the work spaces. Abovestairs, no one should see the busy workers in these rooms or on the backstairs or in the rooms presided over by the personal servants.

If service were to falter, the collapse would start Belowstairs. Her mother-in-law had rebuffed Liza's early overtures of help so sternly that she didn't offer after her first month. When Liza mentioned her management of Corbett Towers, Mrs. Myers' nose pinched in. "I am chatelaine here," Amabel Myers asserted then preceded to order her oldest daughter or Victoria Pethbridge to perform her duties.

Clarissa had tentatively asked a few questions of Liza, more often in the last month than earlier, but she did so secretly. At sixteen, Cassandra should have been schooled in the management of a great house, but she apparently was escaping those lessons.

When Winston opened the door to the housekeeper's office, Mrs. Grunby looked up. He stepped aside. Her black-button eyes widened when she saw Liza. The woman quickly closed a ledger and stood. The petite woman wore a paler grey than the servants wore, and the color blended into the wall behind her. Tugging down her folded-back cuffs, she hastily buttoned them. "Ma'am, I didn't expect you to come Belowstairs."

The housekeeper's gaze shifted behind Liza, at the butler by the door. She gave a brief nod. Liza wondered what Winston had managed to convey without words.

"May I express, ma'am, for myself and all the house staff, our glad thanks that you were not injured earlier? The event shocked us all. I understand Dr. Chambers has seen to your injury?"

"The merest scratch, which we will not make much of, please, Mrs. Grunby." As she approached the desk, she gave another glance around, hoping for a quick read of the woman. Mrs. Grunby had remained, taking reduced salary, while other servants had left Montford. Mrs. Myers respected the housekeeper's opinion, and Winston considered her an ally. Liza knew nothing more.

Providing a glimpse of green and azure, the high window behind Mrs. Grunby's desk had no curtains. A rug, too faded to reveal its colors, covered the bricked floor. Desks gave indications of their uses, but Mrs. Grunby's had a cleared surface except for the ledger on the blotter and a glass inkstand with a quill. Beneath the window stood a three-shelf bookcase with neatly stacked ledgers and looser papers. A couple of milk-glass bowls and an oil lamp sat on the top. A painting of overblown roses in a gold vase decorated the wall, but it would give no indication of the housekeeper's taste, for her back was turned to it.

On the right-side wall, where the housekeeper's gaze could see it, was a child's sketch of trees and a pond. That drawing might hint at Mrs. Grunby's personality.

Liza stepped sideways to view the drawing. The trees were clearly willows, their pliant branches swayed by a breeze. "Is this the pond above the irrigation weir?"

"Yes, ma'am. Clever of you to know that."

"Not clever at all, Mrs. Grunby. When Mr. Myers came to Sheffield in April, he left a plat of the estate with my grandfather. I confiscated it immediately and spent days poring over it, as it gave a glimpse of my new home." Yet on her arrival, she had discovered that her study had served no purpose. Her husband's tour of the estate had been as abbreviated as the one his mother had ordered the housekeeper to give her.

Past disappointments wouldn't rule her life.

"Fancy you recognizing it without the building there, ma'am."

"The artist has a love of willows, I think." She hoped the comment would elicit more information.

"Look at the rock at the bottom left."

She saw the initials, worked to look like the lines of the rock, which wasn't rendered as well as the trees. GDM. "My husband's work?"

"Done when he was just a youth, back on holiday from his school." Pride filled the woman's voice. She had known the young Greville. She had liked him enough to keep this spare rendering. This was the reason Mrs. Grunby lingered through the estate's poorest years.

"And he gave this to you?"

"In a roundabout way, yes," an answer that opened several avenues that Liza wanted to explore. The housekeeper stepped from behind her desk to offer her own seat. "Would you be seated, ma'am?"

"I will not usurp your place, Mrs. Grunby," Liza said firmly, hoping the woman heard the inference about her position. She took the straight-backed chair opposite the drawing. As she waited for the housekeeper to resume her seat, Liza saw a second chair on the wall beside the door. Above it was another sketch, the skill level greatly advanced. Old cathedral ruins, with a tree clinging to a tumbled wall. She didn't recognize this location. "Do I see another example of my husband's art?"

"No. The master hasn't attempted drawing since his father discouraged it."

That answer offered another labyrinthine exploration, yet once more the woman's tone didn't invite questions. One day, perhaps.

"I like this drawing as well, much more than the roses behind you," she decided to say. This time the housekeeper wasn't to be tugged into a confidence.

Mrs. Grunby folded her hands on the blotter before her. Her hands repeated her neat appearance, the nails clipped, the skin not chapped by rough work, but her knuckles showed a few knots from long use. "Mr.

Winston tells me that Mr. Myers gives to you the reins of the household and the meals, ma'am."

She heard a warning although no sign appeared on the woman's stoic face. "Indeed. He quite pleased me with that decision. I ran my grandfather's house for close to fourteen years."

Surprise shattered the stoicism. Her eyes widened. "Goodness, ma'am, you must have been a child."

"I am not so young as that, Mrs. Grunby. I was twelve. My mother was—." Not wanting to mention her mother's difficulties, she altered her explanation. "My mother deemed I should learn household management. I confess, for the past months, I have missed having a finger on the pulse of the house."

The stoic expression returned. "For any mistakes, ma'am, the master knows the reasons."

"I intended no slights, Mrs. Grunby. I know those hiccups came not from your management. But I do not come to speak of the past. Our focus is the future. While I wish to consult with you, I will depend greatly on your experience to maintain the traditions and habits of Myers Montford. If you foresee any difficulty, perhaps my assistance will smooth matters."

The housekeeper's brow constricted. "Then I do not understand the reason the master gives the keys to you, ma'am."

That statement opened an unforeseen difficulty. As long as her mother-in-law retained the keys, Liza did not truly control the house or kitchen. Greville would have to ask his mother for the chatelaine's keys, for she wouldn't. "I believe he hopes for a gradual transition from the dowager's hands to mine."

"A gradual transition? Surely he knows—." She stopped, biting the tip of her tongue, wise reticence.

No doubt, on Mercy's visits Belowstairs, she likely said enough for the both of them. While her maid wouldn't gossip about her own mistress, she would chatter about their past to win confidences to share with her.

Did Mrs. Grunby think her new mistress had thrown a tantrum to get the household reins? *None of them know me yet. They soon will.* On a whim, she changed her approach, using Greville's focus on the land to win her point.

"My husband's chief concern is the estate. I don't think he had realized I had not even a wink at the household management here. Nor do I think he cares, as long as he has what he needs, whether that be his meals or clean shirts or ink and fresh quills. He certainly doesn't understand the labor necessary to maintain this house. Just now, as I spoke with him in his study, I noticed that the fabric on that sofa has worn thin. That is not something either you or I will permit."

At the word *study*, Mrs. Grunby's eyebrows rose, for she knew how few people were permitted in Greville's private office. Liza was permitted while his own mother never ventured past the door, a fact that would sway the woman.

"The sofa in his study? The fabric?" The woman looked perplexed.

"Quite worn and frayed at the corners. I believe my husband's man of business meets with him there? I do know that when Mr. Davenport rides over, they discuss their plans there. I am determined to replace that disgraceful fabric. I believe we also need new table linens. And my husband requests that the china for the tea service be replaced."

"My requests for new linens and a new china service have been denied, ma'am."

"New linens," she said with a firm nod. "We have not the time to replace them before the fête, unfortunately. I understand we host a dinner for our neighbors on the eve of the fête. Do we offer rooms for those who are far afield? What is the state of the bed linens? In three weeks we shall be having frosts, and more than a light blanket will be necessary."

"Yes, ma'am." The housekeeper's faint voice revealed that Liza moved a little fast for her to process. "About the sofa, ma'am, the master will not approve its removal."

"True, for my husband does not like to be inconvenienced. I have learned that about him. But I do not appreciate something so worn and stained remaining in a room that people outside the family will see and use. Myers Montford is the largest estate in this district. The house must reflect our wealth without flaunting it. Mended linens, no matter how fine the stitching, chipped china with mismatched cups, and frayed fabric—none of these are not acceptable, not to me and no longer to my husband. He called me 'the lady of the house'," she shared, determined to solidify her persuasion. "Since I am lady of Myers Montford, wife of Greville Myers, the house reflects my decisions from the point of our marriage forward. Do you understand, Mrs. Grunby?"

The woman's tightly-spaced eyes stared. Then she unfolded her hands. Opening a drawer, she withdrew a sheet of foolscap and a quill. She uncapped the glass inkwell then dipped in the quill and poised it over the paper. "New table linens?"

"I understand the dining table can be extended."

"That is Mr. Winston's purview, but in the past we have hosted twenty-four."

"Will you discover the necessary length from Winston?" In a few minutes they had discussed new linens for the dining table's full extension as well as additional linens for the table at half-length, using a woman in the village to turn an old tablecloth into Battenburg lace mats for breakfast trays, new china for the dining service, and new curtains for the drawing room and the dining room. "I have a china service, still crated in the box room, which we can put into immediate use. The full service for twenty-four, with two epergnes for the table. My husband would like for it to serve for our daily teas. If we cannot receive a china service before the upcoming dinner, we can also use that. Mercy will help you locate the service."

Mrs. Grunby nodded and finished writing. She laid the quill on the rimmed inkstand. Once again she folded her hands. Her eyes lifted. Her thin mouth offered a small smile. "I believe we will not need to replace any bed linens. I would wish you to go through the linen cupboard with me, at your convenience, ma'am. As we have talked, I've considered the difficulty with the master's sofa. We could just replace the cushions."

"Mrs. Grunby, I believe that's our solution! The fabric on the sofa arms is not frayed. We can use a plain fabric to match the older fabric then keep our eyes open for a new sofa. Taking our time, as it were."

"Yes, ma'am. Mrs. Myers," she added.

The housekeeper's first use of her married name gave Liza an unexpected warmth, as if the house staff finally began to accept her rightful position. Where Winston and Mrs. Grunby led, the others would follow.

Liza rose. "We've plans in motion, which always gives me a tingle of excitement. We are not splurging but restoring the house to its rightful position in the shire. Its place was not lost, I think, but not kept forward in people's minds. In previous years, careful management has been the dowager's watchword, but with my marriage to Mr. Myers, we can venture out a little. We can restore the house to its rightful fame, just as Mr. Potts has restored the maze."

The housekeeper's smile steadily widened as Liza spoke. "Exactly so, Mrs. Myers. I believe we shall work well together." Then the smile faded, and a little frown re-appeared. "I do have one concern, ma'am. It's the new maid that Mr. Winston hired. We lost Hobbes, an upstairs maid, two months ago. I hadn't replaced her. When I was ill last month, a young woman came looking for work. Mr. Winston hired her, on a probationary status." She stopped, and the frown increased. "I don't quite know how to say this, Mrs. Myers."

"May I guess that something about this young woman has perplexed you?"

"You have it, ma'am. I can't put my finger on the difficulty. She does her work without question. She causes no problems. She has a quiet way with her. But something—I don't know, ma'am. I'm in a quandary about her."

"You hesitate to remove her from probationary status?"

"It was luck we replaced Hobbes so quickly."

"Shall I interview her then?"

"I would appreciate it, ma'am. Would tomorrow morning at eleven serve?"

Liza would have to use the small sitting room. "That time is suitable, Mrs. Grunby."

After her interview with the housekeeper, Liza visited the cook. She left Mrs. Timmons smiling over the next week's menus. The woman had had little scope for her talents since she was hired in February. Liza admitted to her own excitement over improved meals with more variety.

Going upstairs to remove the blood-stained day gown, Liza ticked off her accomplishments. The staff knew she intended to have an active role in the house. Her goal and theirs would be the return of Myers Montford to its place as chief estate, which meant not just refurbishing and replacing the broken and worn but also opening the house to visitors. As she claimed her position as lady of the house, her mother-in-law would transition to the dowager's status.

More importantly, she had a glimpse of her husband's past interests and talents. The housekeeper's loyalty had kept her employed through the last scrimping years.

Changes were afoot. All because an urn had nearly killed her.

Chapter 6

Although Potts threaded around the parapet surrounding the double-hipped roof, Greville stopped to survey the view.

From this height and distance, the fences didn't need new rails and stone walls hadn't heaved out stones. Buildings didn't need new thatch. Doors and windows and foundations didn't shout with the need for repairs. The boards of the weir race might not hold through winter, but he couldn't see their decay. Swans sailed serenely across the pond dammed by a weir, newly repaired in May—when he should have been greeting his bride on her arrival.

He saw success as well. Cattle and sheep dotted the pastures. Plows turned up dark clods of still-rich soil in the harvested fields. Workers had scythed down grain and now returned to shock the stalks while a hay wagon worked along the hill, the men tossing up forks of dried grass. The money he had plowed into the estate since signing the marriage agreement last January had returned a hundred-fold in the on-going harvest. If the harvest stopped this very evening, he would still be farther ahead than he'd been since taking the reins of Myers Montford.

Hope had returned to the estate—because of his marriage to Elizabeth Corbett.

Liza, he reminded himself.

The lawns and pastures barely hinted at autumn. In the parkland and dotted through the windbreaks and copses, a few trees had jumped the season and displayed the crimson plum of the English oak, the golds of the field maple and black poplar, and the bright orange of the sweet chestnut. They warned of the coming cold, but frosts this year would not catch Montford with crops still in the ground. After a decade of fighting the change of seasons, he wanted to celebrate this year's transformation.

Because of Liza and the money she brought into their marriage.

"Don't you resent her?" Victoria had asked in the first weeks after Liza's arrival.

"She's saving the estate," he retorted.

Victoria had flounced away, as displeased as a child denied a treat.

Deep contentment grounded him every time he opened a ledger no longer bleeding red or talked with his workers about improvements going forward. He'd stopped the juggernaut of decades of mismanagement. Self-sufficient prosperity offered its hands. He even had hopes of buying back the unentailed land that he'd sold to raise funds.

The first year that he served as steward for his missing brother, he'd written to Mr. Vincent for a draw on the principal. The man had arrived to lay before him the limited range of the estate's finances. Greville's threat to contract with money-lenders had sent the conservative solicitor into palpitations. Only the threat had wrung money out of the old man's tight fists. That small injection paid for repairs that kept the farm viable. Every year after, Greville pared expenses more and more in order to endure the estate's shrinking proceeds. With an eye to the future, when he must provide his sisters' dowrys and continue to fund his mother's living, he dared not broach the principal.

Liza's marriage settlements meant no more danger to Mr. Vincent's health, no more contraction of resources, and no more suspension of his plans to recover self-sufficiency.

"Sir!"

Potts's call returned Greville to the roof and the reason they braved the chilly wind.

The head gardener waited for him. Potts stood at the corner with an urn on its pediment behind him. If the old man tripped or backed up a step, he would fall three floors to the ground.

Greville traversed the narrow walk between the double-gables of the roof. The two roofs created their own problem with drainage, fixed early in his tenure with a metal gutter that directed the water away from the inner slopes of the roofs. That stopped the leaks into the second-story chambers but had taken money that should have replaced an outlying barn. Wood planks over the gutter created the walkway to the parapet. Slate tiles butted over the edges of the metal. Everything looked to be holding without problems. No leaks had returned which meant the fix had held. He still begrudged his Georgian ancestor who had demanded the double-hipped roof. When he had more money ahead, he would hire another architect to design a change to remove the problem entirely. For now, though, the gutter worked.

Potts had vanished, walking around to the area above the side terrace. Greville glanced at the other pediments holding urns. He saw no signs of crumbling masonry. Nor did Potts when he joined him, but he said nothing until Greville finished running a hand over the square surface.

"I see nothing, just these scrapes here. These are scuff marks. They got grit in them. Look you. The edge here got scraped a bit, sir. 'Tis in good shape, though. Didn't fall on its own."

The scuff marks backed the man's assessment. "Pushed off," Greville surmised.

Pott's sharp nose sniffed, as if he hunted prey. "Exactly. Weren't no accident."

Greville rested a hand on the low wall of the parapet. The bricks were solid. He leaned over and stared at the terrace. The debris and dirt had vanished, but the shattered paving stones identified the location.

"Took a hard push to move it, sir. Here's one scrape. Here's another. Look here, this edge here——." He rubbed the back edge of the square pediment. "There's been rain on this, like from that downpour last Sunday."

A different color marked the break in the gritty lines. The first push must have prised the urn from its position. The second toppled it over.

"No accident," he repeated. "Someone didn't just bump into the urn and knock it over."

"Not bloody likely, beggin' yer pardon, sir. Take a hard shove twice, once to start it, second one to end it."

"A man? Or a youth?"

Potts' mouth twisted to one side. Once again he scented the air. "Woman could do it, if she put her whole body into it. If she wanted it enough."

"Wanted it? Wanted what?"

Beetling sandy brows drew down. "Your wife's death, sir."

"Potts." Greville searched for words. "That's animus. Hatred."

"Aye, sir."

He examined the next urn. He gave it an exploratory push. He expected Potts to warn him with "Careful, sir," but the gardener waited mutely for him to reach his own conclusion.

The urn resisted his first push. The second rocked it a little. His third push had force behind it, and the urn scraped across the pediment. He didn't need to throw his whole strength into the attempt.

The cause of the urn's fall was only one problem.

He wanted to turn away from the second problem, the one that Potts had pegged—someone wanted to murder Greville's bride.

The second problem led to a third, just as necessary to be solved. Was the act premeditated or the urge of an instance? Had someone seen Liza walking alone and decided to shove the urn? Or had they come up to the roof for the sole purpose of pushing the urn, hoping it would smash her?

A planned murder depended on knowing her location as well as how long she would be there. This attempt at murder depended on chance.

Or did it? For Liza often spent time on the terrace after she walked her terrier through the gardens.

Whoever wanted her death had to know how Liza's concentration blocked out everything around her. He remembered her wave when he rode back. Her brown study came afterward. What had snared her attention?

Did that answer matter? The murderer had seen her distraction and gone to work.

"That little dog saved her," Potts said, tracking one thread of the many coursing through Greville's mind. "I'll not be fussing over him as much now."

"You shouldn't fuss over him at all, now that he has a proper leash."

"No, sir. I mean, aye, sir. What do you want me to do?"

"You found nothing else up here? You came up earlier. Is it as clean now as it was then?"

"Found nothing, sir. More's the pity. I'd like fine to get a hand on whoever did this."

He remembered the roof access through the crowded attic. "Who keeps the key to the box room?"

"To the roof? It ain't kept locked. Nor the box room neither."

"Is there a key?"

"If there be, Mr. Winston's got it."

Or the key hid on that jumbled ring in Greville's desk. "Let's keep the door locked in future."

"That'll hurt your sister Miss Myers some, sir. We see her up here most ever day."

Clarissa? Greville remembered how his sister liked to sketch the vista before she attempted another landscape. She often walked the parapet. On a fine day, she often spent an entire afternoon on the roof. *Would Clarissa—?* He stopped the thought before he completed it. No, Clarissa wouldn't want to murder his wife. Nor would she have lurked around the urns and pushed one off by mistake, not realizing Liza was below.

Cassandra, though—*No.* He refused to suspect either of his sisters, even though his younger sister was too much in keeping with Victoria Pethbridge.

Then he remembered the different-colored scrapes, where rain had washed part of the pediment clean. The first scrapes had occurred days ago, before the weekend rain. The second scrape came this afternoon.

Liza had ventured out with her dog, and the murderer had rushed up here to await his chance. Or *her* chance.

One murderer? Two working in concert? He didn't know. At the danger that none of them had realized, a chill washed through him.

The doctor had intimated the culprit would have scratched hands, but a well-applied shoulder could have easily moved the urn. One good shove, the urn tipped over, and the deed was done.

"Sir? What are your orders about these urns?"

"Let's remove all of them, Potts."

The suggestion didn't surprise the man. Without hesitation, he asked, "You want anything up here replacing them?"

"Later. If at all."

"Mrs. Myers your mother won't be pleased." Greville winced at that truth, but Potts drove on with his point. "She ordered them red cranesbill. Fair run my boys ragged in high summer keeping them watered."

"My mother will understand the necessity of the removal. We want no more accidents."

Those sandy brows came down. "That what you're telling, sir, that it was an accident?"

"I believe we'll say that the pediment gave way. An accident implies a culprit, wholly unintentional but still guilty. Let us not talk of other options."

Potts scowled more fiercely. "The young Mrs. Myers must take care, sir. Somebody wants her gone."

He met those sky-clear eyes, a shock in that weathered face but clearer sighted than most of Greville's retainers. "The urns come down, Potts. If anyone asks, say that the pediment gave away. I will personally warn my wife to be alert."

"Aye, sir."

Greville re-negotiated the narrow walkway between the angled slopes of the two gables then stepped through the access door to the box room.

The servants quartered in the other gabled roof. Storage had filled this attic space for decades upon decades. A broken mirror still in its gilded frame leaned against stacked trunks. He remembered when Stanton had broken the mirror. "Seven years' bad luck," he had crowed at his brother. He hadn't considered that the bad luck would translate into Stanton's murder.

He winced at that memory of his brother's death and the earlier memory of a unthinking child. Ever since Stanton's body arrived, returned to Montford by Agatha Helmes, Greville's memories of his brother were knotted up with the knowledge of his death. For years he had thought Stanton had merely wanted to escape his responsibilities. Burdened with onerous debt and deepening responsibilities, Greville had begrudged his brother's escape. He envisioned Stanton in a warmer clime, happy and free of care. Instead, Stanton's body lay hidden beneath a stair. No one had even known of his murder.

He wished his brother still lived. He wished Stanton did live that idyllic life he had one described, on a Mediterranean island, basking in the brilliant sunlight, his every need catered by an incarnation of Aphrodite.

He wished every memory of Stanton wasn't entangled with the knowledge of his brother's death.

In the close attic air, dust motes drifted. Light shafted through dormer windows, glancing across the storage and offering dim shadows. Covers had slipped off furniture. Paintings grimed with age were stacked together. Someone had pulled away the dust cloth covering a frizzy-haired ancestress in a starched lace collar as stiff as her gown. Several boxes were stacked near an open crate, its packing strewn over the floor. Beyond it were trunks on their ends. The trunks near the narrow stairs were newer, and he guessed those belonged to his wife.

"Six trunks," his mother had protested the evening of Liza's arrival. She had ordered him into her sitting room to voice her complaints. For once, the muck covering him had earned no censure. She had exclaimed at his appearance, so he described the repairs to the weir. Yet he had barely finished before she began her criticism of the new Mrs. Myers. Greville had wanted a bath before re-uniting with his wife. His mother and Cassandra had delayed him while Victoria sat at the escritoire to copy a letter.

He listened and bit back a retort that he hadn't married a pauper. He wanted to point out that his wife brought her entire wardrobe rather than her needs for a brief visit. Some blessed angel stopped his mouth. As his mother grumbled, he'd looked up to see Liza standing in the hall, just beyond the open door of the sitting room. As she approached, he wondered how much she could hear of his mother's complaints. He noticed that his wife lacked his sisters' gliding grace. She wasn't clumsy; she just didn't float like an airy nothing.

Looking back, he realized that he hadn't greeted her with a smile, and she hadn't offered one.

He'd made multiple errors that first day. Elizabeth Corbett had given him one look, down then up, but she didn't comment on the mud smearing him. Nothing in her expression changed. Nor did she greet him. "I had the freight men place my spinet in the library," she announced. "Will there be a more appropriate location for it?"

Before he could answer and remind Liza that he enjoyed her playing, his mother had objected. "The library is inappropriate."

"She can place it in the drawing room."

"Certainly not."

Liza's gaze hadn't wavered from him. No entreaty left her mouth. Until that minute of that hour, he hadn't realized how mobile her features had been in January when they met and in April when they married. And since that minute of that hour, he'd seen her carefully controlled expression on multiple occasions.

"A sitting room?" she suggested. "Or the first-floor gallery?"

"Nonsense," his mother began.

"The spinet will fit in the music room. It opens to the drawing room. When we have guests, they enjoy the music. The music room also has its own entrance, off the hall that leads to my study. We have a pianoforte. I will be pleased to hear you play. It must be tuned, however. My sisters chose not to master the instrument."

"May I send for the man who tunes my pianoforte at home?"

He nodded. "Of course. Now, if I am to dine with you all, I must wash away this grime. A half-hour," he told Winston and ran up the stairs.

With the dust motes drifting around him, Greville rubbed the brass lock plate on one of his wife's trunks. *How did I not see my mistakes?* He cursed the lost months. How many more would have passed, cementing the wall between them, if the urn hadn't crashed down?

The shards of the broken mirror reflected movement. He turned.

Potts climbed into the attic and shut the door to the roof. He started when he saw Greville and yanked off his floppy-brimmed hat. "I'll get my boys onto them urns first thing tomorrow, sir."

"Do that, Potts."

The gardener tugged his forelock then headed down the stairs.

As Greville followed, a flash caught his eye. The mirror's shards had fragmented him. He remembered his boyish glee at his older brother's mistake: "Seven years' bad luck!"

They had missed Stanton for ten years, before his corpse was found secreted in a burnt-out cottage. Another murder, a successful one for it was kept hidden for years. Time and lack of evidence meant that his murderer remained unpunished. For the rest of his life, Greville would wonder who had killed his brother.

Malice drove murder.

Who had hated his brother?

Who now hated his wife so much that she had to die?

Chapter 7

Greville blamed his sister Cassandra for the awkward dinner. "Stop asking Liza how she feels."

"I find it instructive," his youngest sister declared. "In times of crisis, I will know that this is how the merchant class reacts."

Seated across from his two sisters, his wife winced, a reaction he saw only because he worried about an aftershock to her. "Cassandra," he warned.

"I suppose you think you would have had hysterics," Clarissa countered her younger sister.

"I would have fainted when I saw that urn toppling toward me."

"And died," she snapped. "Liza had enough sense to move."

Liza picked up her knife and cut another bite of the beef tournedos. "I had no idea it was falling. My attention was on Sparky."

"That dog!" His mother added nothing more.

Greville eyed his mother, holding down the other end of the table. Not for the first time he wondered if she had no real understanding of the reason he had married. He had explained their straitened finances several times in the last three years. He expected that even his sisters should understand, but his mother and Cassandra behaved as if he were rich as Croesus and hadn't needed any funds to support them or the estate.

"You were ever so calm, Liza," Clarissa said. "If you hadn't fainted, I would never have known you were affected."

"Is that what people mean when they say someone has great aplomb?"

"I believe I was in shock." Liza leaned back and placed her hands in her lap. She sounded calm, but she still looked very pale. "When I lifted my eyes from the urn, I was surrounded by people. Sparky was barking and people were talking—. I remember Greville coming toward me but little more."

"Do you not remember telling Winston to send for Potts?"

"No. Maybe. I confess, my memory is blurred."

"I would prefer that we no longer discuss this," his mother declared. "I think we have wrung sufficient drama from the event."

"Have we?" Clarissa countered. She leaned forward to look around

Cassandra. "Greville, what did Potts tell you?"

That scratched pediment filled his memory. He hadn't decided what to share that information with his sisters. Liza would need to know. Thinking the fallen urn was an accident would make everything simple, but he wouldn't lose his wife and then wonder for years who had killed her—the way he did about Stanton. Steeling against his mother's displeasure, he shared, "Potts agrees with me that all of the urns should be removed."

"What? I particularly selected those flowers. The cranesbills match the banners for the fête."

"Nevertheless," he started only to have Liza support his mother. "The urns give a grace to the roof." His sisters chimed in with their own protests.

He raised a hand to stop the clamor. "Potts will begin the removal tomorrow. I must ask that no one go to the roof until he has completed the work."

"But I always walk the roof," Clarissa declared.

"So do I. Mama does, too."

"I have not recently."

At his mother's comment, Greville narrowed his eyes. This very Monday he'd seen her on the parapet, admiring those red flowers. That was after luncheon. Victoria had trailed behind.

His mother lied. *Why*?

She met his gaze without a flicker of consternation.

Had she gone up to the parapet today? Surely she wasn't strong enough to move that heavy pot filled with dirt? Dr. Chambers said strength was needed, but a woman could shove over the urn.

His mother's hands didn't look marked. She wore lacy fingerless gloves. If her hands were scratched, surely she would wear full gloves? He couldn't see her shoving the urn with her shoulder, the way a workman shove a load.

Nor could he see her attempting murder. *Call it what it is*, Greville ordered himself. Someone had shifted the urn on an earlier date, long enough ago that recent rains had washed the pediment. Once into position, the urn would be easy to topple over. Great strength wasn't needed for that final action.

Am I looking for one person or two? Someone who acts alone, driven by a secret hatred of Liza? Or did one person shift the urn while a second shoved it over? A man and a woman? Two women?

Who would his mother have enlisted as her accomplice?

Had a servant shifted the urn at his mother's order? Surely even the most naïve member of the staff would realize the danger of shifting an urn off-center. Had she enlisted a young footman? Did that unknowing accomplice now fear what the lady of the house had ordered him to do? Or had she enlisted someone else? Someone who admired her? Someone who listened to her resentments about the jumped-up daughter of a mill merchant marrying the master?

"Greville," his mother snapped. "I don't like your expression. Kindly remember where you are and whom you are with."

He didn't know what his expression must be, but he could see the knife clenched in his hand, his knuckles white. He dropped the knife. Deliberately, he leaned back and shut his eyes.

Only to recall Liza frail and helpless in his arms.

Perhaps I should tell them the truth.

"Quite the brown study," Clarissa murmured. "What are you thinking, Grev?"

When he opened his eyes, he fastened on his wife. Fear hadn't paralyzed her. She looked pale, not blanched of courage. She sliced a bite of meat but never carried it to her mouth. Several uneaten bites were pushed about her plate. Had she eaten anything?

Did she suspect attempted murder?

She never lifted her gaze as his sisters continued their complaints about the parapet.

"I started a sketch yesterday," Clarissa informed him. "Without going to the roof, I will not be able to finish my sketch. This means that I cannot offer a watercolor at the fête auction. I swore I would no longer offer my needlework. Last year my tapestry sold for a paltry four shillings. I worked on it for weeks and weeks."

"Six shillings is a week's wage for a laborer," Liza murmured.

"Exactly. And I spent weeks and weeks on that scene of the church. Only Vicar Pethbridge had any interest in it. He purchased it for his study." She rolled her eyes.

"Who did you want to purchase it?" Cassandra asked. "Did you think Richard Davenport would? He did flirt with you at dinner the night before."

"We didn't flirt!"

"I should think not." His mother paused for the plates to be removed. "You are not out, Clarissa. Mr. Davenport's brother is too old for you. Until you are presented to society, we must have a care for your reputation. Greville's hasty and unwise marriage—." She stopped abruptly.

"Do continue, Mother," he said silkily, but she compressed her mouth and met his fierce stare with her own.

As his temper increased, Liza touched his hand.

The gesture froze him. Never before today had she initiated any touching between them.

"Our marriage *was* hasty." She withdrew even as he reached to return her clasp. She smiled, but her eyes remained hooded. "To meet in January and marry in April, that shows great haste."

"Pooh." Trust his younger sister to lower the tension. "Society marriages happen that quickly. Meet in April, marry in June—or in September. I will love going to London. We will have new gowns for day and evening. We will go to parties and balls. We will shop every day."

"Surely not every day?"

"Of course we will, Rissa. We will buy a frippery every day. On Bond Street. And we will drive in Hyde Park in a phaeton!" The last idea thrilled her the most. "Mama, will we be presented at court?"

"I will have enough to do securing vouchers for Almacks. The years that we did not attend the Season have limited my contacts. The death of the countess's mother means that she will still be in mourning next Spring, unable to sponsor you at court. Do not grumble, my dears. You will have plenty of opportunities to meet suitable young men. You need not depend upon a young man that you meet locally."

The footmen moved about the table, setting a quail with watercress before them.

Clarissa wiggled in her chair, as excited by the talk as her younger sister. "I am so looking forward to my first season. Did you enjoy your London debut, Elizabeth—Liza?"

"I did enjoy my weeks there. So many shops and the latest styles."

"But you obviously didn't take." Cassandra had the scorn of youth. "Even with the fortune that my brother found so attractive."

Her smile faltered. "Even with that."

"Sandy," Clarissa huffed, "the questions you ask! Learn a little circumspection. You should be concerned with your own debut, not with someone else's."

"Well, I am not a diamond of the first water, like Victoria, but I do think I will have a circle of admirers. I have a circle here. Mr. Salisbury and Edwin Reade and Marcus Farrow."

Her sister's laugh pealed. "Three admirers do not make a circle."

"How would you know? You have none. I must have admirers in London. My wedding will be the talk of society."

Her mother nixed that idea with one statement. "You will marry from our own church."

"Then I would love an autumn wedding. Mama, do you think I could marry in October?"

"We shall see. Your groom, whomever he will be, will have a voice in the matter."

"If he wishes to marry me, he will bend to my wishes."

"That is not the way it works," her mother countered while her sister cried, "Sandy! Only a man who is stupidly in love with you would accede to your every request. And he would be stupid to fall in love with you."

"Clarissa!" her mother snapped.

"Clarissa! That's so unfair! Mama, tell her not to say such things. When I have my debut, I will still be young. You will be one-and-twenty, Rissa. Old and old. Everyone will wonder why your debut was so delayed. More than three years! People will gossip."

"Enough, Cassandra." Greville didn't like silencing his sister, but she strayed into the offensive.

She plopped back against her chair. "I only said the truth! She cannot say that the man who loves me will be stupid. That will not be true. Why can I not say the truth? She *will* be one-and-twenty. I will barely be eighteen. People will wonder why you delayed her debut."

"Enough."

"But they *will* wonder, won't they, Mama? They will wonder why she did not take. They will *speculate*." She infused the word with innuendo. Her eyes gleamed at the prospect of gossip. "They will look at Clarissa and then look at me and see I am younger and prettier. They will think she lost her beau or strayed or—."

Clarissa sprang from her chair. In her rush to leave, she knocked the table. Her wine glass spilled, staining the tablecloth. She pushed past the footman belatedly opening the door for her.

In the silence after her departure, the clinking of plates at the sideboard echoed.

Greville waited for his mother to rebuke her youngest child, but she merely sipped her wine. Winston moved to refill the wine, but Greville stopped him with a lifted finger. "Cassandra, go to your room."

"What?"

"You heard me."

"Greville," his mother began, but Cassandra spoke over her. "I only asked a simple question. I said people will wonder at the reason Clarissa did not have her debut at eighteen, as I will have mine."

"You implied that your sister was a lightskirt."

"I did not! Besides, when they see how rigid she is, they will know that is not true. Then they will wonder why our debut is at the same time. I do not understand the reason you are so stubborn about that."

"Cassandra, you know the reason. I explained each year when Clarissa asked—begged to have her debut. We hadn't the money to afford a season."

"But we have the money now," she retorted, "because of *her*." She didn't look at Liza, just pointed.

With her head bent, hiding her expression, his wife looked as if she wanted to sink through the floor. She swallowed visibly then offered, "People will understand your brother had to marry an heiress to afford a season for you both. They will not gossip about Clarissa or you. They will sympathize with your brother."

"I should not have to leave," Cassandra insisted. "And they will take one look at you and truly sympathize with Greville."

"Pity would be a better word," his mother chimed in. "They will see the chances he missed."

He could not order his mother to her room. That inability hardened his voice when he repeated his demand. When Cassandra remained seated, he ground out, "I gave you an order."

"Greville. You promised to leave the discipline of the girls to me. You are not to interfere."

Whatever expression now rode his face, she blanched from it.

"I will not interfere, Mother, when you direct my sisters in good behavior. Cassandra, however, has said several things to her sister and now to my wife that will not go unpunished."

"But they are the truth! You cannot punish me for the truth!"

"I do not intend to punish you, but I will remove you from company until you understand that rudeness is not tolerated. You have offended family, and family must stand together against the world."

Cassandra's mouth opened and closed twice. Tears sparkled, brightening her pale blue eyes. "Family? You say *family*? You are protecting *her* over us."

"What are you—?"

"I only want the truth to be said. But it never is, is it?"

"Sandy, don't."

"You don't! Don't call me *Sandy* when you hide behind lies."

"You think I have lied to you?"

"You married *her* in a rush. I thought it was a great love, but you barely talk to her."

Winston quietly ushered the footmen out. Greville didn't quite understand his sister's attack. How had this escalated so quickly? "I explained the reason for our marriage. I told you all, as I have told you for years, that a marriage into money would be necessary to restore—."

"Why did it have to be *her*? She's not us! When we get to London—."

"You may find your debut delayed if you continue this," he threatened. "Do not blame my wife for your childish inability to control your tongue."

"Again! Once again you are picking *her* over us! We are your family!"

"Liza is my *wife*."

"Better for us if the urn had not missed her."

His fist slammed onto the table. China and crystal rattled. "Enough!" he roared. "Go to your room! When you can see your error, you may inform me by a letter expressing your apologies to Clarissa, to my wife Liza, and to me. Only when you have done that will you be allowed to rejoin the family you have insulted."

"Mama—."

"Do not turn to our mother and think she can intercede. Good God, Cassandra! Have you no sense at all? Her wealth provides the food on this table. I could not have afforded the harvest this year without the marriage settlements. That debut you so carelessly talk about will be funded by Liza. That very dress you wear—."

"Don't you dare tell me that she paid for it!"

"She did."

Cassandra shoved back her chair and jumped up. She jerked at a sleeve. "She can have it!"

"Cassandra!" The double note of shock from their mother stopped his sister before she tore the gown. "This behavior is appalling. Your brother requested that you retire for the evening. Please do so."

"But Mama—."

"Be so good as to honor my request, Daughter. Think on your relationship with your sister. I think you did not intend to hurt her feelings. Nor did you intend to argue with your only living brother."

"No, I did not. I only want people to stop hiding behind lies."

"Go to your room, please. I will speak with you later."

Cassandra hesitated. Her head almost turned to Greville. Then she clenched her fists and stalked to the door. She fumbled with the knob. The door opened, the footman on the other side swinging it wide. Head up, she sailed from the dining room.

Chapter 8

Greville had no doubt that once Cassandra reached her room, she would yank off her gown and toss it into the hall. How many days would her tantrum last? The one last autumn had continued for three weeks. All he had done was deny her request for a riding horse to replace her faithful Nell, grown too old for more than plodding along the lanes.

Winston returned. "Sir, should I serve the next course?"

Liza gave a sharp inhalation. He didn't miss the lift of her chin, the squaring of her shoulders, as if she prepared for another battle. After Cassandra's attack, did his wife expect an attack from her mother-in-law?

"Yes. Winston, see that Cook has a tray prepared for Miss Myers."

"And Miss Cassandra," his mother added.

"No, not my younger sister."

"Greville—."

He tapped his fingers on the table. "One hungry night may help her see the error of her behavior."

"I do not accept that. You wish to punish her for insulting your wife."

"Did you not hear her, Mother? She wished that urn—."

"I heard her," she cut in quickly, "but you know your younger sister. She can be overly dramatic when she is thwarted."

"*Overly dramatic*," he repeated. "That is an understatement. She might have learned to control these histrionics if she were not overly indulged."

"I do *not* indulge her. You yourself have heard my reprimands."

"They have no teeth, Mother. You give an edict, but you do not enforce it. I daresay you will not only sneak food to her—."

Those Valkyrie eyes opened wide. "I will not go against your wishes."

"No, you will have your maid do it. You will also dictate her letter of apology. I will not have that. I forbid it, Mother. That letter needs to come from Cassandra herself."

"She may need a little guidance with the wording."

"I forbid it," he snapped, but only Liza flinched at his harsh words.

"Cassandra needs to learn her errors and accept the consequences. If I do receive a letter from her on the morrow, I will know that you dictated it."

"Will you let her starve?"

"She only misses the last of her meal," he pointed out. "I know how stubborn she is, but we cannot bend in this, Mother." He heard the plea in his last words and wished he could retract them.

Too late. His mother also heard the plea. Her mouth twitched, already anticipating how she would circumnavigate his order.

And Liza's shoulders sagged. Here was the battle she had anticipated, the clash of wills with his mother. He understood her reticence to insert herself into this family fray, but he wished she would fight beside him.

Did she think he would give in to Cassandra and his mother?

Insight blinded him. Just as he knew so little of her, she knew little of him. She didn't know that he wouldn't cave. How could she know? He'd spent the summer months more involved with the estate than with his family. He'd let his mother rule the house. He'd let his mother and his sister talk around Liza and refer to her in pronouns rather than with her name.

He wanted Liza to fight beside him.

She had no idea that he would fight beside her.

.~.~.~.

Liza had squirmed through much of Cassandra's prattle. Greville's lively younger sister did not usually chatter, nor did she so openly attack her sister. She usually contented herself with digs that flew past her brother, for his attention barely focused on his family. Her comments tonight, however, almost sounded prompted.

She didn't know whether to celebrate Greville's awakened attention or dread it. Since she had roused from her swoon—*faint!* the practical Liza chided—his solicitous attentions had rent her calm in twain. Delighted and apprehensive, she confessed to additional surprise from Clarissa's behavior. She liked the older of his two sisters. Tonight, she hurt for Clarissa, a physical throb that created salty tears in her throat. Cassandra's attacks had visibly hurt her older sister. She had fled rather than take another barb.

Would Greville have stepped forward to discipline Cassandra if Clarissa hadn't flown from the room?

What had driven Cassandra's venom? Did she not understand the dangers of her insinuations about her sister? Her anger had blown up like an unexpected tempest. What fed that storm? Thwarted hatred?

The shattered urn flashed, red flowers and scattered dirt and broken stone.

When had Cassandra reached the terrace? Liza could remember the arrival of Winston and Clarissa. She remembered that someone had taken Sparky in the house. She had bled, but she hadn't felt the scratch or the blow from whatever caused it. The cut throbbed now, reminding her with every pulsebeat of Death's bruising touch.

We have the money now. Because of her.

Cassandra's stabbing finger had pierced Liza's heart. She knew whose resentment fed those words. That antipathy was born before Liza arrived at Montford. The only son had sacrificed himself, and the mother despised the symbol representing that sacrifice. Liza's delay in arriving had likely raised hopes that she would remain in Sheffield. Then she arrived and disrupted their little idyll. Cassandra's enmity, all unknown, had also festered.

When Liza spoke up, she had hoped to dissipate the escalating emotions with a bit of reason. She only earned Mrs. Myers' seething retort. When Greville didn't defend her, Liza deflated. Did the Myers women want her absolute silence? Was her complete absence the only thing that would restore their contentment?

She didn't retreat. She had vowed not to attack. Never before tonight had she found it so difficult to listen to the argument and remain silent.

I am the cause of their argument. The admission hurt. She had endured Grandfather Corbett's tirades. She would endure the coldness of these women.

Greville had asserted that she was *family* in a voice that reverberated to her bones. She wanted to bask in that brief minute. Yet while his support filled Liza with warmth, it had sparked a fire in his sister, who accused him of lying.

Amazed that Mrs. Myers hadn't sent the servants from the room, she signaled to the butler to return to the kitchens. She had no illusion about staff's loyalties. They would support only what the master did. The lower ranks would take their cues from the butler, the housekeeper, and the cook. If Greville supported Liza, the servants would obey her. If he did not—.

And then Cassandra wished the urn hadn't missed her. Even as she gasped with the pain of their hatred, Greville roared—and her heart resumed its beating.

She gaped at her husband, filled with energy, an aura expanding his body. She couldn't hear his words. She could only drink in the power emanating from him.

In January, his reticence hadn't impressed her. Used to her

grandfather's blustering and bustling, she found the gentleman hesitant and ineffectual. *No wonder his estate is failing around him,* she had thought. *I will control my destiny with this man.*

For years her mother had complained about her subjugation while living at Corbett Towers. More than once, Liza pointed out that Mrs. Corbett had only to chose the life she wanted for Grandfather to provide her the funds. Her mother had refused—*Oh no, dearest! I cannot abandon you.* On marrying Greville, Liza asked her mother to come with her to Montford, to escape Adam Corbett's house.

"Not until you've been married a full year, dearest."

Liza hadn't understood her mother's refusal. Now she looked at her husband and realized how little she knew of him. Worse, she understood him not at all.

She would never control her destiny. She could either partner with him, or she could be swept behind him, tossed by the waves whenever he surged. She might set up her own establishment, but she would forever be tied to him.

And her foolish heart wanted to remain here, near him, even when he acknowledged her importance only once a week.

Her grandfather's bluster and bustle didn't match to Greville's elemental force. He had restrained his true power until this moment, hiding it with good manners that were only a veneer.

Greville didn't lie, not the way his sister claimed. Liza had met liars. They tried to hide their lies by accusing other people of the deed.

Who did Cassandra think had lied? Not Greville. Not herself, surely? Her mother? Clarissa? Who else could Cassandra mean?

Once more the shock of the falling urn assaulted her.

She blinked and realized a footman had served the next course, a green sallet. The dish that she and Cook had changed would follow.

Liza peeked at Greville. Tension surged around him, exhibited by his scowl. His disagreement with his mother had sounded like no more than a conversation, but undercurrents seethed. She strove to see deeper than the rushing upper waters. He understood his mother very well, but he seemed not to see her antagonism toward his wife. *How does he not see it?*

That urn had done much more than focus his attention on Liza. It had shattered the façade that covered Cassandra's antagonism. It scattered additional debris that broke whatever had hidden his mother's hostility.

Liza shouldn't rejoice.

Almost, almost she heard concern in Mrs. Myer's voice when she queried, "Will you let her starve?"

"She only misses the last of this meal. I merely confine her to her room. I know how stubborn she is, but we cannot bend in this, Mama."

Liza winced, for the words held a plea. Mrs. Myers smirked at his weakness.

The sallet was removed, untouched. The next plating would be the apple crumble that had replaced the custard. The egg dish had slowly cooked most of the day only to be drowned by a kitchen maid.

Small bowls with spoons for the caramel sauce were placed to their right hands. Then the footmen placed the individual ramekins filled with apples baked in egg with nuts and sugar, a simple crumble. Winston moved around the table, pouring a wine to complement the sweet.

Liza tensed.

Mrs. Myers spooned up the caramel sauce. She let the creamy liquid stream from her spoon onto the apple crumble.

Does she not notice? Does she not know?

When Liza had spoken with Cook, they discussed a replacement for the ruined dessert then moved to meals for the weekend and next week.

She picked up a spoon. Ignoring the sauce, she took a bite of apple. Tart sweetness bloomed on her tongue.

"Cook is changing my menus again. I specifically ordered a steamed pudding." Mrs. Myers didn't mention that Clarissa had communicated the demand. "If she can forget a recipe in one season, she is no longer useful."

Greville put down his spoon. "Mother, about that."

"Mrs. Timmons cannot go a single week without changing something. This is insolence."

"I am certain she had a reason."

"She always has a reason. She makes the change with not one word to me. I hear only her reasons on the next day and nothing more."

"I do not understand the difficulty."

I have to say something. Liza placed her hands in her lap and stiffened her spine. If Greville had remained that elemental force, she would have dove in without a qualm. His plea to his mother had returned him to a hesitant and ineffectual gentleman.

"I spend much time developing meals we enjoy and that Cook is capable of preparing. If she cannot—."

"Pardon me," Liza interrupted. "Mrs. Timmons is not the problem. Her staff creates most of the problems. Tonight's custard was ruined when one of the kitchen maids poured too much water into the cooking pan."

The silence that followed her explanation hurt just as much as Greville's roar had.

Mrs. Myers meticulously returned her spoon to its place. "May I inquire as to how you know this?"

"I spoke with Mrs. Timmons earlier."

"Mrs. Timmons blamed a kitchen maid for the custard's failure?"

"The girl was in tears. She had never before had charge of a custard cooked in a *bain marie*. She was afraid that Mrs. Timmons would fire her."

"Mrs. Timmons cannot keep staff?"

"No, I did not say that. I believe today was the first time that Eliza Jane helped with a steamed pudding. She was hired in late April."

"I see," Greville said, her last statement a clear explanation for him.

"You obviously understand what I do not, Greville," Mrs. Myers complained. "Please enlighten me."

"I authorized Mrs. Timmons to hire additional staff when I returned from my April visit to Sheffield. After my marriage to Liza."

The older woman placed her napkin beside her spoon. "Cook's staff was previously inadequate—." She didn't finish.

"As I explained repeatedly, we did not have the funds to pay for the complete staff she requested when I hired her in February."

"You did not inform me."

He sighed as heavily as he had at his sister's willful misunderstanding. "I told you, in November, that our problems were more serious than simple economizing. I explained the debt. Father had increased the mortgage. I worked for years to pay more than the interest, but my efforts were never enough. We fell behind two years ago. I explained all of this. You chose not to listen. You have complained that I cut luxuries. I didn't. We were barely subsisting."

She blinked. Her chin lifted. "Stanton would never have run the estate into the ground."

Liza pricked her ears. She rarely heard any mention of Greville's older brother. She knew he was deceased, or Greville wouldn't have inherited. The manner of his death, the reason for his long absence, those she didn't know.

"Stanton was as profligate as Father for years. I thought one reason for his disappearance was his debts in London, debts I had to cover when it was clear he would not."

Mrs. Myers pressed her fingers to her mouth. The action was a pretense of fighting a sob, yet her eyes remained dry. "You should not speak ill of your brother."

"Perhaps, as Cassandra said, we should stop hiding behind lies and speak the truth. Stanton ran up a tremendous debt with his gambling and wines. Only the best, he would say, and that ran from beaver hats to leather top boots. Paying his debt required a small fortune, everything I had set aside for my sisters' debuts. My fault for not making you listen when I explained that Clarissa's debut would not occur."

"We could have gone to London—."

"I have a great dislike of adding to the debt my forebears accrued."

When compressed tightly, Mrs. Myers' lips disappeared. The tight seam of her mouth separated her pinched nose and pointed chin. "You *had* to marry her then?"

"As I have explained. To your benefit. To my sisters' benefit. To my own benefit." He cast a heavy frown at Liza. "I have yet to determine if my wife receives any benefit from our marriage."

"She has the benefit of our name," his mother snapped, "and the proud heritage attached to it. Both of those outweigh anything else."

Still looking at Liza, Greville twisted his mouth, not quite a sneer, definitely not a crooked smile. "While the past informs our future, I am discovering that the past is much less important than the future."

"I do not understand you, Greville."

His gaze returned to his mother. "No, you never have, and I find no benefit in re-hashing what will always be an impossibility. We were speaking of Mrs. Timmons and her kitchen staff. I know that you find interactions with the cook tedious, especially since she replaced Mrs. Mosgrove. Who was worn off her feet from trying to run the kitchen with only two girls to help her. You complained about Mrs. Mosgrove's meals, have you forgotten that? You have also complained of Mrs. Grunby's faults, complaints that would likely dissipate if you unbent enough to have personal interaction with our staff. They answer directly to the lady of the house—yet I know that you require Clarissa or Victoria Pethbridge to act for you. My wife, however—."

"I never said that I would not interact with staff."

"You choose not to do so, Mother."

"Clarissa needs to learn to manage a great house. When she marries, she will be expected to assume the reins of the household."

"At the moment, all Clarissa is learning is to run your errands."

"I will teach my daughters, just as I taught Victoria. I expected you to marry Victoria, not this grubby-handed mill worker's ugly daughter." Liza flinched at the triple insult. Mrs. Myers bored on. "Victoria expected it as well."

Liza stared at her husband, wanting to see his reaction.

At his mother's accusation, his gaze flicked to hers, but his mask remained, hiding his emotions. Greville flattened his hand on the table. Then he looked at his mother from under his brow. "I gave Victoria no promises. I was careful not to speak of commitment or the future whenever I found myself in her company."

"Victoria rejected several marriage proposals in the hopes of yours."

He shook his head. "I can hope the sun will shine during my morning ride, but I place no expectation in it. Victoria was free to make her choice. Just as I did."

"Your choice was *her*!"

Liza jerked. When her mother-in-law barked a laugh, she wished she had controlled the reaction.

That ugly burst of noise had destroyed Mrs. Myers' veneer of elegance.

As gently as before, Greville asserted, "My wife's name is Liza. As you have abrogated your responsibilities as lady of the house, Liza will shoulder them."

"Her? You think her shoulders are wide enough for those responsibilities?" Her mocking tone grated just as the laugh had. "She does not know anything about being a Myers of Myers Montford."

"She will learn. I had hoped that you would assist her learning, but you have chosen another path. So be it. She managed her grandfather's house in Sheffield, a larger manor than ours. He entertained a great deal, I believe, and the house's staff is double the size of ours."

"Not quite," Liza said faintly, determined to avoid any semblance of a lie.

His mother drew herself erect. Her mouth stretched, a rictus that destroyed her beauty. "You will tell me next to remove to the Dower House in the village."

"If that is your wish, Mother, I can assign staff to have it ready within the week."

"That is not my wish!"

Mrs. Myers' wine glasses rattled when she slapped the table, but nothing else did. She lacked Greville's roar. Her active strength removed, she would be more dangerous than before, striking like a snake from cover.

The older woman signed to a footman, peeking in from the hallway. He dashed forward to draw out her chair. When neither Greville nor Liza moved in response to her obvious withdrawal, her scowl deepened. "I have finished dining."

"We have not, Mother. I wish to finish this excellent dish before me. What is it, Liza?"

"Apple crumble."

"Simple but still excellent. You will share my enjoyment with Mrs. Timmons?"

"Of course." And she picked up her spoon.

His mother huffed and stalked out, her back as rigid with

indignation as her youngest daughter's had been.

Chapter 9

"Leave us." Greville ate another bite of the sweet dish.

He didn't speak as the servants filed out of the dining room.

At Greville's right hand, the butler placed a snifter with an inch of its bottom filled with a dark amber liquid. Then he poured Liza a splash more of the cabernet. Both served, Winston eased from the room.

Her husband ate more of the apple crumble while Liza cast for something to say and hooked nothing.

"You said very little," he murmured.

"My few words only provoked more issues. I was not certain that I should enter this battle."

"Battles." He stressed the plural. "Cassandra's truths were certainly spoken tonight. We hide too much. We do not tell lies, but—."

"We mask the truth."

"Mask. That's a good word for it, isn't it? A smiling face for everyone while we dam up a flood of emotions. I wish you hadn't such forbearance. I wanted to roar with anger when Cassandra said ... . I'm masking again, aren't I? I cannot believe my sister wished you dead."

She flattened her hand beside her plate and stared at her neatly-trimmed nails. It hurt to hear those words aloud, as if thoughts could be ignored and easily forgotten. "You did roar."

"You should have screamed."

"To what purpose?" That reeked with bitterness. Deliberately, she lightened the next words. "That would only confirm my lack of gentility. No, thank you, sir. My grandfather visited much worse on my head. I learned to endure his tirades then continue with what I wanted."

His hesitant smile surprised her. "Can I expect that from you in the future? To have you blithely sit through my temper then go about quite merry after I have stomped off?"

"I was neither blithe nor merry. Nor can I believe you would scream and stomp around." Liza offered a shy smile. "You called her bluff."

"My mother? Yes."

"Cassandra's as well."

"Perhaps. Cassandra is more uncontrolled than I realized. This day has awakened me to much that I was missing." He leaned forward to clasp her hand. The heat of his surprised her. "Good Lord, your hand is ice." He picked it up and chafed it between his.

She dared not ask about Victoria Pethbridge. Tonight, from Greville himself, she had learned more than in the five months of asides from the Myers women. Mercy had reported the staff gossip. Greville had spent over a decade holding the estate for his elder brother. If he had inherited earlier, long before he discovered Montford's straitened circumstances, would he have married Victoria?

The young woman was lovely. Even with jealous eyes, Liza admitted that she had a beauty that would endure. She had attempted to befriend Victoria. As vicar's daughter, she would know more people blanketed by her father's ministerial care. Rebuffed at the manor, Liza had hoped to involve herself in the parish. The women of the church, however, followed Mrs. Myers.

Would they change once they learned of the changes at Montford?

To avoid talking about Victoria, she cast a different direction. "What did Dr. Chambers mean, Greville, when he talked about injuries to hands?"

One eyebrow quirked, a trick she wished to master. Leaning back, he lifted the snifter and swirled the brandy, warming it with the heat of his hand. "What you do you think it means?"

"He thinks someone pushed over the urn."

"Exactly. Potts agrees, but he thinks the urn was shifted last week, before our last rain. It would have needed only a good shove to fall over."

"Our last rain? That was five—six days ago."

"Premeditation."

"But that would be murder! Who would do such a thing? Did they not see Sparky and me below them?"

"Liza—."

"Good Lord," she whispered. "They wanted to kill me."

And she remembered that Clarissa had said she would have screamed *murder*.

.~.~.~.

That night, as they came together, Greville lingered as if he wanted to tempt words from her. Afterward, he buried his face in her neck. Liza could not mistake his reluctance to leave, but she couldn't guess what he wanted. Words of affection? Of love? To talk of love would be one of Cassandra's lies. He had to know her respect for him. He had crossed a bridge today, a transition that marched from caring toward affection and might lead to love. She had tended the last crumbling wall around her heart for so long that, should he breach her last defenses, he would conquer her heart.

She did relish his new awareness of her as his wife rather than the woman he had married for her money.

She cupped his nape, cradling him closer. Wife. Husband. Wasn't that enough for now? Yet when he removed from her, she felt bereft.

"Tomorrow, Liza?"

"Yes?"

He stalked from her room to his and swiftly shut the communicating door.

As she washed, she considered those two words. Were they a question? Or a simple statement? *I don't understand him.* Since the falling of the urn, he had changed, and in changing himself, he changed their roles, just as he had changed her role at the manor.

Sparky pattered around, his sleep disrupted until she climbed back into her bed. Then he yawned and returned to the pillow and blankets kept for him in her dressing room.

Liza slept uneasily, waking, remembering, shivering with fear rather than cold, shivering with apprehension for the coming days.

.~.~.~.

Saturday, 4 September 1813

While she'd finished her first cup of tea, as Mercy heated water in the kettle over the fire, Liza mulled over the person who must hate her enough to want her dead.

Cassandra had announced it. Mrs. Myers might agree to it. Victoria Pethbridge? Someone unknown?

She remembered Greville's delay in coming from the stables. He was last to appear.

What had delayed him? Had he gone to the roof?

He defended her to his family—surely that belied any desire to kill his rich wife.

Widowed and still wealthy, he could marry Victoria, the best of both worlds—the money he needed, the woman he desired.

But last night ... . Was he lulling her into a security until she fell into his next snare?

.~.~.~.

After breakfasting in her room, Liza wrote three letters. When she ventured downstairs, she handed them to Winston for the daily post. In the letter to her mother she poured out her emotions and apprehensions.

Not wishing to worry Deborah Corbett, Liza still wanted relief from some of her repressed worries.

She burnt that letter when Mercy left, jumping back into bed when the maid returned. Mercy sniffed the air, gave Liza a stern look, then bustled into the dressing room. Liza composed a better letter to her mother, describing only *a lucky escape from an unfortunate accident* then detailing the changes Greville had initiated. She crowed a little over her status as lady of the house. With no one else could she celebrate that change.

Her second letter she wrote to her grandfather. She informed him of the fallen urn, but she did not call it an accident. She did write *lucky escape*. In her account of last evening's dinner she included Cassandra's damning *Better for us if the urn hadn't missed*. As she read over the bald recitation of facts, she nodded. It said what she wanted. Her grandfather would also read everything she didn't say.

The third letter contained much the same information as her grandfather's. That letter would find its way to her own solicitor's desk.

The door opened. Liza didn't turn from the library window overlooking the forecourt. A groom cantered his horse along the drive, heading for Wellesbourne Montford. The strap of a mail pouch crossed his back, a white slash against the drab cloth of his shirt, like the bar sinister across a blank armorial shield of old. She watched until he rode into the parkland then looked over her shoulder.

Winston waited. He bobbed his head once. "Mrs. Grunby, ma'am, said that you would interview the new maid."

She remembered. She also remembered that the butler would have tucked her into the small sitting room rather than risk a battle with Mrs. Myers. After last evening, listening to her husband deal with his sister and then his mother, Liza wanted to avoid her own battle. It would soon arrive, however, for she would need the desk in the larger sitting room for the accounts. "Remind me of her name, Winston."

"Tillie Sparrow, ma'am."

She skirted around the table with its atlas and globe. "Where have you placed her?"

"She waits in the hall, ma'am. However, the elder Mrs. Myers has sent word down that her personal items are to be removed from the large sitting room. If you wish, we can clear the room in a half-hour. The dowager sent these as well." He produced a ring filled with keys.

Liza took the chatelaine keys, retained by the lady of the house, as Greville called the position. She sorted through them, small, large, darkened by age or shiny with use, with no organization for their placement on the ring. The bits of several keys gleamed in the sunlight flooding through the library windows, especially the small one that would fit a desk. "Are these the housekeeper's keys?"

"Mrs. Grunby has a different set, for the areas she is responsible for. As does Mrs. Timmons."

The housekeeper would have keys for all of the private chambers as well as the staff rooms, the china closet and linen cupboards, and other storage spaces as well as any supply cabinets. Cook would have keys to the spice and sugar chests, the pantries and scullery, the smokehouse and the pottager shed, the last which the head gardener would also have. Winston had keys of his own, for the silver and the wines and more.

Liza would have preferred Mrs. Myers turn the keys over with her approbation and guidance. That would never occur, not after last evening. Without last evening, though, Liza might never have received the keys.

Yet this morning, her mother-in-law cast off her control, obedient to her son's command. How much had Greville surprised his mother last evening?

"Did my mother-in-law have any other changes for you?"

"No, ma'am. The dowager did send word that she would partake of luncheon in her room."

"I see. Was a tray provided for Miss Cassandra this morning?"

"She refused to open her door. The maid left the tray for her."

"And Miss Myers? Where is she?" Liza doubted her mother-in-law would help her discover the lock for each key on this heavy ring, but Clarissa would know many of them, having used them to perform her mother's errands.

"Miss Myers is riding with the master, ma'am."

Greville rose early for his morning rides. Clarissa rarely joined him. She wondered what they would discuss.

But she had delayed over long. Winston waited for her to move forward. "I will interview the new maid in here, Winston. I believe I can find paper here."

Instead of directing her, he crossed to the ancient monastery sideboard centered beneath the great library windows. Opening a side drawer, he produced several sheets of foolscap which he placed on the central table. His second task brought over the inkstand from the small table tucked against the cornering bookcases. He checked the quill then pulled out a chair.

She set the keys beside the papers. "Thank you, Winston. I do have one request of you. Would you oversee the placement of a few of my personal items in the sitting room? My maid Mercy will provide them. Nothing much, just touches of my own, you understand."

"Of course, ma'am, as it should be. Do you wish me to remain for this interview?"

"I do not believe that is necessary. I have interviewed servants since I reached thirteen years. Mrs. Grunby asked that I conduct this interview. She trusts your decisions, but I am discovering that she places prudence first."

Something changed in his face. She wasn't exactly certain what that was. He didn't smile, but the dourness eased. "Mrs. Grunby is a careful housekeeper, ma'am. You show wisdom in listening to her little cautions. They may seem unlikely, yet I have found them extremely useful."

"Then we are of the same mind, Winston."

"Yes, ma'am. You should find the large sitting room available for your use within the hour. Shall I send Tillie Sparrow to you?"

"Please do so."

When he opened the library door, she saw a footman passing through the hall, carrying under his arm a rolled carpet in shades of blue and green. She almost called back the butler, but a young woman entered.

"Mrs. Myers. Ma'am." She bobbed a curtsey.

"Tillie Sparrow."

"Yes, ma'am."

"Please, shut the door, Sparrow, and sit here." She indicated the chair across the table.

As the maid complied with the first order, Liza took the opportunity to form a first impression. Tillie Sparrow looked enveloped by her apron, tied at the back with a large bow. She looked neat and trim, her hair hidden under a mobcap. Her white cuffs, turned down for this interview, were crisply starched. Even her shoes, on view beneath her dark skirt, were buffed to a high shine.

She came to the library table, but she didn't draw out the chair. "If you would not mind, ma'am, I would rather stand."

"As you wish."

The maid kept her eyes downcast, properly subservient. She had clear skin, a little pale from indoor work but of a smooth quality that bespoke care as well as youth. An artist would be enamored of her bee-kissed mouth.

Was the young woman's beauty the reason that Mrs. Grunby hesitated to remove her probationary status? The footmen would fall over themselves to impress her. Licentious male guests might impose upon her. Her beauty might tempt Greville.

Yet he'd withstood Victoria Pethbridge.

How many positions had the maid lost because the lady of the house became jealous of her beauty?

The maid looked up, revealing deep blue eyes that a susceptible man would drown in.

Liza re-arranged the papers that Winston had placed for her. Taking up the quill, she wrote *Tillie Sparrow* across the top. She refused to fall victim to prejudice. "Do you know the reason for this interview?"

"Mrs. Grunby said that she'd rather you make the decision about new staff. She's hesitated over it for more than a fortnight now. Ma'am."

"Do you have any thoughts about her hesitation?"

"No. Ma'am."

"You brought references?"

For answer, she reached beneath her apron and into a capacious skirt pocket. She drew out a long flat pouch. Using the table, she opened it and produced two letters. A third remained folded in the leather pouch.

Liza opened the first letter. From Hinkley, Leicestershire. A spidery hand that hinted at age had signed *Mrs. Cuthbert*. She had little to say beyond Tillie Sparrow was an honest and diligent worker. She regretted that she could not remove Tillie with her when she joined her daughter on the coast. The second letter repeated the first, this time from Cirencester in Gloucester. Written by a solicitor named Howard Gartman, the facts listed the maid's employment for six years for an elderly lady. Upon the woman's death, Mr. Gartman had released Tillie Sparrow from employment. His signature sprawled under the neat letters of the reference.

She refolded the letters and returned them. "How long were you with Mrs. Cuthbert?"

"Almost eight years." Once tied, she held the flat pouch rather than return it to her pocket.

"Fourteen years in service, then. How old are you, Sparrow?"

"Three-and-twenty."

"You went into service at aged nine?"

"My mother was cook for Mrs. Cuthbert. When she died, Mrs. Cuthbert gave me a place, cleaning for her personally. My duties extended as I grew."

"You are remarkably well spoken for a maid."

The young woman's eyes flashed. Her lashes swept downward, hiding the emotion that had peeked out. "Mrs. Cuthbert taught all her servants. Begging your pardon, ma'am, but I understand your home was in Sheffield."

"Do you suggest that I am too used to the Yorkshire accent?" She smiled, but the maid kept her gaze lowered.

"As you say. Ma'am."

"What brought you to us? Were you with an agency?"

She took a deep breath. "I have a cousin in Yorkshire. Gilbert Meaney. I believe you know him?"

Liza didn't share that she had once wondered if Gilbert Meaney wanted to marry her—those few precious weeks before her grandfather returned from London and changed her future. "Mr. Meaney manages the mill closest to my home." An up-and-comer, Adam Corbett had called the young man when he visited the house. Her grandfather had several times enlisted Gilbert to squire her to occasions in the city and several dances in the area.

Thinking Gilbert had approval, she welcomed him during Grandfather's absence. He came for tea and stayed for dinner, with Liza's mother overseeing that sedate courtship. They rode together with a groom trailing behind. He held her close during the Christmas waltz. When her mother was distracted, he touched her crimped hair then her lips, briefly and swiftly, before touching his own mouth, the semblance of an innocent kiss.

Grandfather's arrival at Epiphany changed that weak little attraction. When he told her his plans, she ventured to mention Gilbert. He had shouted, "That weasel is all right for running a mill, but he is not for the likes of my granddaughter." Then he stomped from the room. Weeping, she wrote to Gilbert. After she posted the letter, she wished to retract every word.

He never responded.

"I am a little acquainted with Mr. Meaney," she answered Tillie Sparrow.

"When I wrote and told him I needed a new position and couldn't find one in Gloucestershire, he advised me to come here. He indicated that you might be willing to hire a relative of his, that you and he were close for a time."

Liza's cheeks bloomed. *Close* could mean so many things. "Did you convey this to Mr. Winston when he hired you?"

"The butler asked only to see my references. He said Mrs. Grunby would decide to hire me or not, but I would be paid for my work and given room and board until that decision was made."

"I assume Mrs. Cuthbert and Mrs.—."

"Wilton. Ma'am."

"I assume they had smaller households than we have here."

"No more than the three of us at most."

"Elderly ladies would not require disparate chores from you. We will soon have a harvest festival followed by dinners with our neighbors, and then Advent and Christmas are upon us. You may be called upon so often you feel pulled in different directions. Decorating for the fête, serving at table, weaving wreaths and hanging garlands and ribbons, that may not seem part of your tasks."

"I like my work here. The pay is better than I expected."

"What of your fellow servants?"

"I have no complaints. Ma'am."

That belated addition of the respectful "ma'am" was beginning to rasp Liza's nerves. She took a moment to write the particulars of Sparrow's former employment as well as Lawyer Gartman's name and direction, then she laid the quill on the inkstand. "I believe you are currently serving as a chambermaid in the family wing. Do consider yourself no longer on probation, Sparrow. I will inform Mrs. Grunby."

"As you wish. Ma'am."

Liza had thought her words a clear dismissal, but the maid lingered. "Do you have a question, Sparrow? Or a comment?"

"No. Ma'am."

"Then you are dismissed."

She curtsied and left, shutting the library door firmly.

Liza stared blindly at the words she'd written then walked back to the large window that covered the entire side of the room. She didn't see the curving drive, the gardener raking the lawn he had scythed, or the trees leaning with the wind. She remembered Gilbert's touch to her mouth then his. She remembered his sherry-colored brown eyes, the stubborn wave of his dark hair over his forehead. He could speak broad Yorkshire, just as Grandfather did, but he controlled the heavy accent and dialect in her company.

After her failed seasons and three more years with no eligible bachelors brave enough to face Grandfather's wrath, Gilbert Meaney's arrival seemed God-sent. He had treated her respectfully, as if she were fragile china. Used to bossing servants and managing tradesmen, Liza basked in a perspective that considered her helpless.

She couldn't have maintained that helpless façade very long.

Tillie Sparrow pointed up her physical deficiencies, just as did Victoria Pethbridge. Mousy hair, brown eyes, features that were only plain, Liza knew that only money drew interest to her, just as it had carved Greville's path to her. She had admired his honest admission that he needed the funds she brought into the marriage.

Gilbert had pretended an attraction. Greville never disguised what brought them together.

She wished she had burnt that letter to Gilbert. How he must have laughed at her silly dreams.

Chapter 10

When Greville and Clarissa entered the house, piano music thundered along the passage.

"Good heavens," his sister declared, removing her hat and scarf, blown by their long chase across empty pastures. "I did not know your wife was capable of such passion."

Nor did he. Liza usually played light *etudes* or an occasional country dance. She loved music. She'd recently received a piece he particularly enjoyed, for all of its fierce grace. At Corbett Towers he had discovered how well she played. He remembered his surprise that a plain woman had such a sensitive connection to music. Whenever possible, he closeted himself in his study when she had her daily hour of practice.

Last month he had gifted her with several scores for the pianoforte. In her delight at his gift, she approached true prettiness. He dared not tell her that he hadn't selected the music, merely dictated that his man-of-business Mr. Vincent select a variety for a proficient pianist.

Occasionally she returned to the spinet she'd brought with her. While of beautiful woods, it lacked the range and tonal capabilities of the pianoforte. And its thunder. Her practice on the spinet was technically proficient but lacked the emotion she could wring from the pianoforte.

Needing to change his attire, he still headed for his study. The music room was nearly across the hall. As he entered the back hall, the last chords faded and no other composition continued. Sharp regret pierced him.

His wife emerged as he reached the study door. In her haste, she collided with him.

Greville caught her upper arms. "Steady," he warned then saw tears on her cheeks.

Metal clanked to the floor. She gasped. Before she could, he bent and retrieved the ring of keys.

She swiped away the tears. Then she held out her hand.

He returned the keys. He wanted to ask what had so disturbed her, for she wasn't given to tears, but a footman came down the passage. She stepped aside, ready to pass him. He touched her arm. "I regret missing your hour of practice."

Her reddened eyes widened. He had surprised her much more than that simple statement should have. "You listen to my practice?"

"Whenever I can. From the first time you played Mozart, rather than those country dances. Your talent gave me a glimpse of you." Her cheeks pinkened, so he added, "You should play something like Mozart the next time we are in company."

Liza shook her head. "It never does—." She bit her bottom lip. "Not when I am still so new here."

He understood what she hadn't said. "I forget. Our neighbors have daughters who must share their painful attempts at the pianoforte. You are wiser than I, Liza. Yet I would like to show off my wife's skill."

"Like showing off a trick pony?"

That keen question revealed an inner turmoil deeper than mere tears.

Since her arrival, she kept layering on cloaks of reticence. Yesterday had stripped them away. He didn't want her to resume that reserve. Last night, once he heard the animosity voiced by his mother and younger sister, he understood her sheltering cloaks.

Or masks. That word remained appropriate.

The footman returned, empty-handed.

Greville drew Liza aside as the young man passed. Then he drew her through the door to his study and guided her to the sofa. A perplexed frown creased her brow, yet she sat and gazed about her, looking as fragile as the lightweight dimity she wore.

Crossing his legs at the ankles, he leaned on his desk. "What was that music?"

Her frown deepened. Her fingers gripped the faded fabric beside her lower limbs. "It's a piece by Beethoven. His Sonata 17."

"Will you play it again? Tomorrow? Or the next day?"

Her jerky nod mirrored her confused frown.

He hid as much as she did. He never asked what he wanted to. Inside him, something had cracked open, like a new seed. He didn't know what it was. He only knew light gleamed through that crack, beckoning him to prise his way out. He wanted her with him a little longer. "How is that wound you received?"

"Oh." She lifted her arm, as if she forgotten it. The gauzy sleeve of her day gown veiled the flesh, but he could not see a bandage. "I would certainly not call it a wound. Just a cut. It is healing."

"Did you bruise?"

"A glorious angry purple and blue. It doesn't really hurt."

"You are recovered? From yesterday?"

The eyebrows that had gone up descended again. "I only swooned,

Greville. Nothing really happened to me."

He wanted to remind her that someone tried to murder her. "Your music this morning—something has disturbed you."

She looked down, watching her fingers pleat the gauzy windowpane fabric over her lap. "I am angry at myself. At a past foolishness." She rose quickly, teetered on a step, then gave him her back as she walked to the window.

He supposed he should be grateful that she had not left the room. She opened an opportunity to discuss that past foolishness. Unfortunately, he reckoned that it would not be pleasant to hear.

The view from his study overlooked one end of the terrace, a swath of lawn, then the tall hedge that formed the outer wall of the maze. She stared out as if something had seized her attention and, talon-sharp, refused to release her.

He came behind her. She heard him, likely smelled the combination of his sweat mixed with horse and leather. Her neck looked slender, a long column. Wisps of her hair had escaped from the braided coronet. He remembered it last night, falling around her shoulders like a silken cape.

"Liza? What past foolishness?"

"A silly girl's dream. Before I met you."

"And the memory disturbs you?"

She sighed. "Do any of us want to remember past embarrassments?" She turned. He didn't fall back as she had expected. Her revealing color rose, but she didn't retreat. She forced a shaky, little laugh. "I am certain even you have events you would rather not remember."

"Dozens." He snared her hand, the one with the ring of keys. He lifted her hand and let the sunlight play over the metal. "My mother has given you the keys."

"She sent them to me, yes. She is also ceding the large sitting room to my use. That surprised me."

"Watch for poisoned darts."

She gasped, flashed an upward glance, then continued to meet his gaze. "If that is an attempt at humor, husband—."

"A poor attempt, wife." He rested his left hand on her hip. "In bad taste, after yesterday."

Her color heightened again. In the base of her neck, a pulse fluttered. Her face lifted.

Someone knocked on the study door.

He growled and swung away from her. "Enter."

Potts stood on the threshold. He wore the same raveling sweater from yesterday. "Pardon, sir, ma'am. It's the pots, sir. The ones on the roof."

Liza shrank back, which angered him for her sake. Emotion darkened his voice. "What about the urns?"

"We removed the flowers. I can plant them in new containers. They will make a good show by the entrance. But the pots, well, sir, we can move them, just as you want, but it ain't going to be easy getting them down that narrow stair and through the house to the outside."

Remembering the weight of the urns, Greville imagined holes in the walls, shattered plaster and cracked flooring, urns escaping to roll down the stairs and crush anyone unlucky enough not to be forewarned.

"Push them off," Liza advised.

"Ma'am?"

Shocked by the suggestion, Greville looked around at his wife. Sunlight flooded around her, bright enough that it created no shadow on her face. Her high color remained, but she didn't look disturbed. Unlike moments ago, when her fluster had nothing to do with yesterday's experience and everything to do with her husband's intention to kiss her.

"Push them off," she repeated. "Put two of your boys well back from where they will fall, and one inside to keep anyone from coming out unawares. Then just push them off."

"They'll break, ma'am."

She shuddered. "Very likely, but that is preferable to any future accident. Is it not?"

Potts scratched his thinning hair.

"Much more preferable," Greville agreed. "Do as my wife suggests. Explain to the boys how important it is to keep everyone from harm."

"No need to tell them that, sir, not after yesterday. Pushing them over will be quicker, for sure. We can get them down in no time. But, sir, we'll break more of them pavers, and the lawn's bound to get dented and the gravel in the forecourt—."

"We'll do any repairs necessary. My chief wish is to remove the urns as soon as possible, as we discussed."

"Aye, sir. I'll see to it. Ma'am." He tugged the thin wisps falling over his high forehead then retreated.

Like moth to flame, Greville leaned closer to Liza. He wanted to taste the passion she released in her music. "Now, wife, where were we?"

"There you are!" Clarissa cried.

He groaned.

Liza chuckled, almost making up for the lost kiss. She rested a hand over his heart and leaned around him to smile her greeting to

Clarissa. "Did you enjoy your ride?"

"It blew away cobwebs and all sorts of poisonous spiders. Rather, Grev's sharp words commanded them away. I came to find you, Elizabe—Liza," she changed, with a deprecating moue, "because Mother says she gave you the chatelaine keys. I know you will be curious about which keys fit which locks."

"I *am* curious. And afraid I shall be confused for some time."

"You will learn. I did. Believe it or not, there is a system." She held out her hand as Liza neared then linked their arms. "Never fear. I shall rescue you."

"Clarissa," Greville stayed them, "Is that what Mother said? That she gave Liza the keys?"

"Actually, she said quite a bit more, but as you commanded, I choose not to listen to deliberate venom. Now Liza," she drew her into the hall, "the first key is the one that unlocks the desk in the sitting room. You should make changes there, I think, first of all."

He heard their conversation continue down the hall through the still-open door. He realized that Potts hadn't shut the door when he left. He would have kissed Liza in view of everyone passing. And he didn't care.

It *was* that cracking seed, he decided as he ran upstairs to change his riding clothes. It caused crazy thoughts.

Like his preference for Liza over Victoria.

He'd never lost himself with Victoria. In her company he never forgot open doors and sharp-eyed servants.

Last summer, when Mr. Vincent broached the estate finances, he had also produced a list of four ladies with fortunes suitable for marriage. Greville had rejected the list, thinking the quarterly interest would keep Montford from drowning in the River Tick until harvest came in. Unexpected expenses drained the quarterly before he touched it. By then, one of the four ladies had married and a second was betrothed, both to fortune hunters like himself. The third was ten years old than he. If he had to marry, he wanted a son to inherit the land he struggled to save.

He was considering the fourth lady when Adam Corbett offered his bargain and twice the marriage settlements. Briefly, he wondered if an indiscretion drove the old man's desperation to marry off his granddaughter. His man of business thought the other lady's family would come up to snuff when they heard of Corbett's offer. Distaste fouling his mouth at the idea of being auctioned off like a stud, Greville didn't present himself for bidding. He released himself from that tentative overture and traveled to Sheffield.

From the first meeting, Elizabeth Corbett surprised him. She wasn't as plain as the old man described. She had gentle manners that proved refinement that the old man lacked. Her speaking eyes and ready color would betray any immodesty. Yet he delayed the marriage to April. If she'd had any swelling to her stomach when he'd arrived then, he would have cried off. She'd remained as slender as in January, a little paler, although she flushed prettily when one of her grandfather's managers had drawn her aside on the day before the wedding.

She still flushed easily. He caught only the occasional flash of her eyes, usually when someone offended her.

He'd expected her to assist with the household management. His mother quickly disabused him of that idea, and the pressing needs of the estate kept him occupied. Working in the fields, he would see Liza on long walks with her dog. He knew she took drives to the village with Clarissa.

Yet after six months of marriage, he still didn't really know her. He wanted to. He determined to do so—if his mother didn't throw up more obstacles.

One of her chief obstacles was Victoria, whom she considered more suitable than Liza.

Victoria was suitable if one only looked at the station to which the Pethbridges belonged. Third son of a baron, the vicar received the living at Wellesbourne Montford, a minor rung in the climb of the church. Greville liked the vicar. He had a true charity for his flock, evinced by his sermons about Christ's sacrifice and glory. As hard as Greville worked to restore the estate, the vicar worked to help the less fortunate in his parish.

His daughter, though, received more of an inheritance from her socially-conscious mother. Granddaughter of a baron, Victoria was several rungs up in his mother's favor. In the last year, though, she constantly exasperated him. She plucked at his sleeve to ask when he would visit or to propose an early morning ride. She pestered him to sit beside her at dinners. She presented her card at the country dances and asked him to write his name three times, then she pouted when he refused. He couldn't call her encroaching, not when his own family welcomed her daily, but he drew a strong line. If he danced with her, he danced with other ladies, married and single. If he sat beside her at a dinner, he engaged all his neighbors in more conversation than with her. He never went riding with her unless Clarissa also went.

Greville knew Victoria had harbored expectations. After they buried his brother and before Mr. Vincent apprised him of the bleeding accounts, he had even considered marriage to her. He never comprehended the exact thing that drove him away from that idea. The way she came to greet him first whenever his family arrived at a party?

The weight of her hand claiming his arm after church services? The dark flicker of her eyes when he talked of helping someone she considered beneath her?

The poison he overheard.

Victoria might fit his rank, but she didn't fit his world.

When he returned from Sheffield to announce his marriage to an heiress, she'd sat beside his mother on the sofa. Her expression remained tranquil as he shared his news. After he dealt with family, she rose and glided to him. Resting a hand on his upper arm, she lifted her face and in a husky voice asked, "You want money that desperately?"

"The estate needs the money," he responded.

Her question "Will you not feel sold, a slave at auction?" first offended him then angered him. Had she not heard, for the past year, all his comments about the estate's needs, needs which only a cash infusion would solve?

"The estate comes first," he retorted.

Blue eyes wide, she looked him up and down as if he were a creature she'd never imagined. Then she walked away.

Victoria's father came with additional questions. Greville guessed that those questions were planted by Victoria although she herself would never ask them. When had he met this Elizabeth Corbett? Had they formed an attachment? Did he not worry about bringing a crass sensibility into a manor long respected for its gentility? Those questions didn't come from Vicar Pethbridge, lost in his New Testament teachings.

Greville refused to answer any of the questions. Nonplussed, the vicar had soon left.

Remembering those questions with their tinge of venom, he wondered if Victoria had used a wickedly forked tongue to poison his family's view of Liza long before she arrived. And on every day since then.

Victoria's daily visits must end. Without her constant injection of venom, his mother and Cassandra might recover from the poison and discover Liza's worth. The change would take time, but it would occur.

Once again he saw that shattered urn.

Victoria had been there, he remembered. She might have prodded Cassandra into a wildness. That might explain Cassandra's behavior last evening.

He hadn't asked enough questions, of the servants, of his sisters and his mother, and of Victoria. He needed to ask those questions, before whoever had pushed over the urn decided their hate hadn't been satisfied.

Chapter 11

Clarissa turned from the drawing room window. "Brace yourself."

Liza looked up from sorting the key-ring, trying to remember the sequence Clarissa had repeated several times. She had trailed behind her sister-in-law for what felt like hours, learning the sequence of keys based on the sequence of locks from room to room. They had investigated the house from ground floor to the attics. She had opened so many locks that her fingers hurt. "I beg your pardon?"

"Visitors approach," her sister-in-law intoned with appropriate gravity. "I believe it's the Pethbridges."

She stared at the keys while she wished she could retreat to her room. She knew what the conversation would be: the urn, her swoon, their speculations and commiserations, and a pithy prayer of gratitude for her safety.

No, she was doing a disservice to the vicar. His heartfelt prayers and earnest sermons always touched her. He inspired his sincere listeners to live as Christ had. His genuineness remained a pleasant surprise.

His daughter and wife, though—.

"The box room," she said, pretending triumph to have identified the three-bit key. Then she crammed the crowded ring into her reticule. She needed to get a girdle for the key-ring, one that would be easy to don and remove. Hoping Clarissa hadn't read her racing thoughts, she joined her at the window.

The drawing room overlooked the expanse of the forecourt and the sweep of lawn to the parkland. The manor's southern exposure, with the bank of windows in the drawing room and the library, admitted considerable sunlight in summer. With no curtains to draw across the glass panes, Liza was already imagining the cold that would come through the windows in winter. The drawing room's massive hearth would barely heat the room on icy days.

She yanked her thoughts from plans for refurbishing the manor and focused on the dogcart rolling along the gravel drive. The driver had stowed the whip and let the piebald horse set its pace. Behind him, sitting on the small benches across from each other, were two bonnets, summer straws with bright ribbons. She'd seen those bonnets before, at the church bazaar.

"All of the Pethbridges," she gloomed.

The mantel clock began striking the hour.

"In time for tea," Clarissa said cheerfully. "That will help pass the time."

"Will you greet them, Clarissa? I need to speak briefly with Mrs. Grunby."

"Of course. Do you think Mama will bestir herself from her self-imposed exile?" She didn't wait for an answer but headed for the door. Liza heard her speak to a footman, directing him to escort the visitors to the large sitting room.

Clever Clarissa, Liza mentally praised. With Liza presiding in the domain of the lady of the house, the altered positions of the two Mrs. Myers would quickly spread throughout the district. Even if her mother-in-law did not keep to her room, Liza would have charge of the tea service. Mrs. Pethbridge's need for gossip would inform the women of the village. Like thistle seeds, the news would spread.

She ventured Belowstairs. A passing maid informed her that Mrs. Grunby was in her office, "with your own maid, ma'am." Preoccupied with the visitors, Liza recognized Tillie Sparrow as she darted away on the words.

She tapped then opened the office door.

Mrs. Grunby jumped up. "Mrs. Myers."

Mercy hopped from her chair. "Oh, miss, miss, it's horrible. Horrible! I don't know how it could have happened!"

"Mercy, what on earth?" Then she saw the broken china scattered across the housekeeper's desk. She recognized the multi-colored flowers and gilt edging.

Wordlessly, she picked up a triangle shard of the china. She had brought the service all the way from Sheffield. Only yesterday she and Mrs. Grunby had planned to replace the manor's chipped china with this pretty set, bought when she'd gone to London for her debut. She'd fallen in love with the painted flowers strewn over the white plates. Gold rims emphasized the elegant shapes of the teapot and cups. Quatrefoil plates and saucers increased the charm of the service. Her grandfather had refused to let her use it, so she packed it away until such a time as she could make her own home.

On her wedding day she had pulled out the dragon-spout coffee pot, a large bowl and a platter, the only pieces she had ever used until coming to Montford. Since then, she'd used a single service with its teacup and saucer, fruit bowl and bread plate, and a side plate along with the teapot. Mercy would not let anyone else touch the service. Liza woke each morning looking forward to seeing the service on her breakfast tray.

Yet while she now had her own home, the Meissen china would never be used.

She set down the flat shard of a plate and picked up the pointed ear broken from a cup. "What happened?"

"It's all like that, miss—ma'am." Mercy touched a curved piece, large enough to be broken from the coffee pot.

"What do you mean? All?"

"Shattered. And it weren't, not before."

"I don't understand."

"Let me explain." The housekeeper's fingers grazed over the broken pieces on her blotter. "Mrs. Mercy and I and two of the maids went to the box room to bring down your tea set, just as we discussed, ma'am. The lid was off the crate."

"The straw was everywhere," her maid chimed in.

"Mercy, let Mrs. Grunby explain."

"Well, ma'am, just as Mrs. Mercy said, a lot of straw had been pulled from the crate and just left scattered on the floor. Then we looked in the crate. It seemed only half-full, and Mrs. Mercy said that couldn't be right, for she had packed it full and tight. I questioned if this were the correct crate. It was the only one opened—."

"I had it opened, remember, ma'am? After we arrived. I got out the little teapot and a single serving set for your personal use. After it were clear that old bi—."

"Mercy."

"She is, ma'am. And I wouldn't 've put it past her."

With a sinking heart that knew already, Liza turned back to the housekeeper. "Please. Tell me."

"When we reached into the straw, we began finding these broken pieces."

"Every piece destroyed," her maid added.

"We went to the bottom of the crate. Every piece is broken."

"As if someone climbed into that crate and stomped and stomped and stomped. Your favorite china, ma'am." Mercy sniffed, as if she were as heartbroken as Liza. "Deliberate."

She turned the cup handle then placed it on the table. She wiped her fingers down her skirt. "Perhaps the china was broken in transport from Sheffield."

"No, ma'am. I had to hunt through that straw to find the lid to your little teapot. I removed several cups and saucers and a platter. You remember that large platter, ma'am, the one what served the meat on your wedding day? Broken in two it is. None of them pieces were broken when I unpacked them. I put everything back careful and neat, with the straw still round it. And I put the lid back on the crate, though I didn't nail it back in place."

"Every piece?" she whispered.

Mrs. Grunby answered. "All except the service that your maid had withdrawn."

"I'll keep real careful with that, ma'am. No one's touched it but me, and I'll keep to that. This is—this is just—."

Malicious was the word her maid needed. Liza tore her gaze from the broken china. "When was the last time anyone was in the box room?"

"That would be difficult to say, Mrs. Myers. The room is not kept locked. The garden boys go through the box room to water the plants on the parapet. Miss Myers goes up to the parapet almost every day."

The parapet. She controlled a cringe.

"We need to lock it," Mercy declared. "What if someone got into my lady's trunks? All them winter clothes I still hadn't got unpacked."

"I suggest, Mercy, that will be your next task. I am certain Mrs. Grunby can spare a maid or two to help you remove the gowns to my dressing room."

"That dressing room will turn into a nightmare, ma'am. I only now got it sorted the way I like. I done brought down your warm clothes, but I was leaving your winter tweeds and heavy coats in the trunks until I set up something to keep moths out of the wool."

"How many trunks, Mercy?"

"Just two, ma'am. I won't need nobody's help to do it, but the moths—."

"I believe two trunks will fit in my dressing room, under the window. Perhaps that can be the solution."

"Sparky likes to lay under that window, ma'am."

"He will have to accept a change, as we all do. There was another crate, with a silver tea service and a Queensware service for twelve, I believe."

"That crate was untouched," the housekeeper added. "Mrs. Mercy thought it would be, for it was still nailed shut, but I didn't feel right not checking it. Nothing there was damaged, and I had the maids bring down every item for washing."

She needed to move on, not keep staring at the broken china that she had loved. "Very good. Excellent. We have visitors for tea, Mrs. Grunby. I had hoped to use—we shall begin to use the Queensware for teas and for dinners. We must move a little more rapidly in our selection of a new dinner service. Two dinner services, one in simple classic lines and the other ornate, I think, both able to mix with each other.'"

"Very good, ma'am. I would have suggested that very idea. I will write to London immediately. What with the fête, we'll need a sturdy service as well."

"I leave it to you, Mrs. Grunby. Mercy will need a strong footman to carry the trunks."

"Alfie can do it, ma'am."

The name was unusual for a footman. "Alfie? Do I know him?"

"He usually works for Potts, but he's been building shelves for me, for my room."

Liza arched her brows. "Shelves, Mrs. Grunby?"

"For my books, ma'am."

Curious, she couldn't stop her question. "Do you read novels? The ones by Miss Austen are very fine."

The housekeeper permitted a smile. "Much finer than some I could name, ma'am."

"We must have a conversation about your favorite by Miss Austen. I wish we could do so now. I would prefer that conversation to entertaining my guests." Dissatisfaction twisted her mouth. "The Pethbridges."

"The vicar's a fine man."

"He is. I enjoy my conversations with him and look forward to his sermons." She turned only to be called back by Mercy.

"You'll not need to be taking that with you, ma'am." She plucked away a shard of bowl that Liza hadn't realized she'd picked up.

"The tea will be served momentarily. I'll tell Cook, shall I?" The housekeeper came around her desk.

Dammed back by sadness then control, Liza released her anger as she climbed the steps to the ground floor. Her fist rode the wall, pounding it with every other step. *How dare they break my china? Who would do such a thing? Who would climb into the crate and jump up and down? Who would delight in hearing china break?*

Someone malicious.

How did deliberately breaking china satisfy any kind of hate?

No, that was the wrong question. The result may have been the china, but the cause—that was directed as Liza. The china was broken because it belonged to her. The intent was to damage her possessions.

And the intent of the toppling urn was to damage her. To kill her.

She wondered when the person had realized the opened crate held her china. The china could have been broken weeks, months ago, and no one had noticed because no one needed to unpack the crate.

Whoever it was would not have the satisfaction of seeing her shock and horror. Only Mercy and Mrs. Grunby had seen her reaction. She couldn't believe either of them had jumped up and down with glee as they destroyed her possessions.

It was the same question, escalated: Who hated her that much?

Her mother-in-law hated her, but Liza couldn't see the woman climbing up and stomping around.

Cassandra would. Yet the young woman's anger last evening was actually directed at Greville, not at Liza. Unless she'd done it days and days ago, long before last evening's argument, long before the urn that Greville claimed had been positioned so an easy shove would topple it.

No proof.

No proof of who had destroyed the china or when the destruction occurred. No proof of who re-positioned the urn or when that occurred. Both events could have been weeks, months ago, as far back as May. Ten minutes would be all they would need for the china. Much less than that for the urn. A quick opportunity seized, and destruction was assured. Chance for the first act, premeditation for the second. Both took the same kind of hate. Both directed the hate at her.

The box room was never locked, to permit the gardeners access to the roof. The heavy thuds this morning had slowly, so slowly tolled off the urns' removal from the parapet.

Should she lock the box room? Especially now that the gardeners would not need to water any flowers. Very soon she would discover who wanted access to the box room or the roof itself.

Who else had a key to the box room? Mrs. Grunby would. Winston? Potts?

Who went to the roof? Clarissa. Cassandra. Mrs. Myers, but she claimed she'd not been up for several weeks. Victoria, accompanying the sisters at various times. On her walks, Liza had occasionally seen servants on the parapet.

And Greville, just last week. Before the rain.

Liza passed through the green baize door and started along the back hall, but she saw herself following Sparky through the maze. Released from the ribbon leash, the terrier dashed ahead of her and soon darted around the corner. She heard him running along the blind alleys, nosing around before he ran back, staying ahead of her as she followed the secret to the center.

He waited for her at the center, with its little bench and statue of a nymph. Tail wagging, he pranced to her. She bent to re-attach the ribbons before starting out. After the last incident with Potts, she didn't want Sparky to earn more wrath. He hauled her behind him. His paws dug into the slippery grass.

When they emerged from the maze, Liza considered her return to the house and balked. Another hour of walking would benefit Sparky and help her sleep. She studied the sky to gauge the likelihood of rain.

A pattering of drops would not curtail their walk, but the late summer rains often soaked her through. She didn't want to venture out without a cloak.

On that day, a flash had caught her eye. At the corner of the roof stood her husband. He didn't appear to have seen her. He gazed at the park. She couldn't discern his expression. Usually somber, he seemed burdened of late by unshareable secrets.

He hadn't stood near the urn that had later fallen.

Yesterday he'd become protective of her. He offered her the chatelaine's position, five months after it rightfully should have come to her, with Mrs. Myers assuming the role of dowager, even if she did not intend to move to the Dower House. He'd alienated his mother and a sister in his support of Liza.

Was that to soothe her worries—and to offer him a mask for his true motives?

If I die, all between Greville and his mother will be forgiven.

If I die, Greville can marry Victoria.

Pain streaked through her, bright and destructive as forked lightning. Liza clutched her stomach and gasped.

"Mrs. Myers?" A footman hurried to her. "Are you ill, Mrs. Myers?"

Dogged will straightened her spine. "Roberts, isn't it? A momentary pang, but I thank you for your concern."

"We have visitors, ma'am. The vicar and his family. They are in Mrs. M—in your sitting room."

His change, strangely, shoved a brace under her. *My* sitting room. *My* house. *My* home.

My husband.

Greville hadn't chosen Victoria Pethbridge. He'd had years for that decision.

Masks, she remembered. He removed his only occasionally. Yesterday. Last evening, when he'd lost his temper with Cassandra. Today, when he leant close to kiss her then looked frustrated when Clarissa interrupted them.

No, surely Greville had not tried to murder her.

Chapter 12

"My dear! Oh, my dear!" Mrs. Pethbridge flapped her hands, an awkward heron in blue-grey ruffles and lace.

Sparky barked then escaped Clarissa's lap. He sprinted past Mrs. Pethbridge and stopped at Liza's feet. He wiggled with excitement until she lifted him, cradling him in her arms while she dodged his cold nose and eager tongue. Holding the dog effectively halted the older woman's advance.

Liza shifted Sparky so he had less chance of licking her face. He shifted to doggy kisses of her hand and wrist.

The vicar stood before the settee. He held papers which he folded as he offered her a smiled greeting. The empty seat beside him was likely his wife's. Victoria had chosen the petit-point seat near the cold hearth, where the unobstructed sunlight would complement her glowing skin above a rich blue pelisse. The top button remained undone, to reveal the blue-and-white cameo she always wore, this time suspended from a yellow ribbon.

Neither her mother-in-law nor Cassandra were present. She wondered what excuse Clarissa had given.

Mrs. Pethbridge stationed herself on Liza's right, away from Sparky's wet tongue. She dogged every step. The older woman seemed non-plussed when Liza took the dowager's upholstered chair. "Is Mrs. Myers not to join us?"

"Not today. She is a little out of sorts." Clarissa exchanged a quick smile with Liza. Only they two knew what *out of sorts* meant.

The vicar's wife returned to the settee. "We are so grateful that you escaped harm. Aren't we, Mr. Pethbridge?"

"Indeed, dear." He looked up from the papers and peered over the top of his glasses. "Mrs. Myers, when we heard of your accident—.

"Hardly an accident," Clarissa countered, "since Liza had nothing to do with the urn that nearly killed her."

"Miss Myers! Surely not? We heard she was on the terrace when an urn fell over—."

"Which urn do you think fell, ma'am?" Liza placed Sparky on the floor. Her eyes caught on the burlwood chair with its brocade fabric, the seat to which her mother-in-law always relegated her. No one deserved that uncomfortable chair, not even for the half-hour of tea. Even as she listened to Mrs. Pethbridge, she resolved to replace that chair with something more comfortable. For now, she watched Sparky, nose to carpet, as he visited every foot in the room.

"After Victoria informed us, we thought a topiary at the entrance had fallen over."

"No, Mrs. Pethbridge, it was a rooftop urn. I am surprised Victoria neglected to give you that important detail." Clarissa wielded a sharp tone. Sparky nosed her. She patted him. His tail wagged as he ventured to the vicar. "The urn shattered on impact and barely missed Liza. She providentially received only a scratch. Our gardener has not yet replaced the paving stones. Would you like to see how they were shattered?"

"A roof urn?" The green eyes shared with her daughter widened.

The vicar removed his *pince-nez*. "Mrs. Myers, you could have been killed." He gave Sparky the same smile he bestowed on all his parishioners.

"Saved by Providence," Clarissa declared.

Sparky sniffed Victoria's shoe. She nudged him away. He huffed then trotted back to Liza where he flopped down on her foot.

"That urn must have weighed more than three stone. It's cast stone, isn't it? Filled with dirt, it would weigh even more. Mrs. Myers, it would have crushed you."

Liza winced. "Believe me, Reverend, I have thanked God for my fortunate escape. I am surprised, though, at Victoria's report. She was here, wasn't she?" She turned to her rival. "You were assisting my mother-in-law with the invitations for the fête, weren't you?"

"I was here. I left after you fainted. I would have thought you would have fainted after it happened, but you were quite calm, giving orders to Winston and Potts."

"Was I calm?" she countered. Was that hostility in Victoria's eyes? "I do not remember." *Did Victoria go to the roof? Did she wait for her moment then rush downstairs before anyone connected the urn to her?*

"Dr. Chambers diagnosed shock," Clarissa inserted, still fighting Liza's battle.

"Victoria told us very little. Mr. Pethbridge was away, visiting old Mrs. Cooper. He returned very late."

The door of the sitting room opened. The tea cart rolled smoothly until it reached the carpet. The china rattled as the maid pushed the wheels over the edge of the knotted-pile Savonnerie rug.

Wanting to swing the conversation away from the urn, Liza caught up the thread Victoria had introduced. "Mrs. Cooper? Is that the lady who sang at Midsummer?"

As she hoped, the vicar caught the thread and rolled it up. "No, ma'am. Mrs. Cooper does not venture far from her cottage. You are thinking of Mrs. Willets. Mrs. Cooper is in ill health."

The maid placed the cart at Liza's right hand. A posy of late flowers from the cutting garden was tucked into a celadon vase beside the silver teapot. As the vicar enlarged on Mrs. Cooper's circumstance, Liza poured into Queensware cups which the maid served around before offering plates with savory tartlets, shortbread biscuits with a lemon curd, and a wedge of spice cake. Mrs. Timmons' choices, for Liza hadn't mentioned the afternoon teas when they discussed the meals. Biting into a biscuit, she vowed to let Cook continue to surprise her at tea.

Sparky toured the room, hoping for crumbs. Clarissa dropped a bite of the mince tartlet. Sparky sniffed then snapped it up. He sat back, watching for another treat.

"Has Dr. Chambers seen Mrs. Cooper?" Liza asked as the vicar wound down his list of the elderly woman's ills.

"My dear," Mrs. Pethbridge whispered, "Dr. Chambers can scarcely afford constant charity. The size of his own family requires a careful hold on his expenditures."

"Does the church have an indigent fund?" She didn't ignore Mrs. Pethbridge; she just continued to focus on the vicar. Sparky planted himself beneath the man's right hand and was rewarded when the vicar swept cake crumbs to the floor.

"You see, Mrs. Myers," Victoria explained, as if she were a child who didn't understand, "the coffers would soon be drained if we constantly offered charity. Even your massive wealth would soon be drained by a wholesale charity."

"I do understand. Yet did not Mrs. Cooper have a position in Wellesbourne before she fell ill? We should assist her so that she may resume that position. As you said, Reverend, she frets that she is so dependent on others. We can assist her until she is returned to health."

"That is Christian charity, but when a woman is sickly most of the year—."

Liza interrupted her rival. She kept her appeal focused on the vicar. "What is her illness?"

"The doctor will not tell anyone." He looked concerned at that, but he did offer a minuscule smile. "Mrs. Cooper is not wholly without assistance, ma'am. The church provides her cottage rent-free, at your husband's request. He sends a box of foodstuffs every week."

"Which she sells," Victoria snapped, a bit of temper slipping past her mask.

Clarissa gasped. "She sells what we send?"

"*We* send it?"

"Greville does," his sister explained. "Mrs. Cooper worked here before she married and had her children."

"She was formerly employed here?" Liza spied a plan to help the woman.

"She worked in the laundry. I believe that, after her husband died, she returned to that work, taking in laundry from her neighbors and others."

"She has children?" Mrs. Pethbridge's downbent nose scented a way to relieve a burden from the parish. "When she fell ill, why did she not go to them?"

Clarissa shrugged. "I think one son has died. I'm not certain what happened to the other."

"He went to the colonies," the vicar supplied, dropping the last of his tart on the floor. Sparky pounced and swallowed with an audible gulp.

"Mrs. Cooper has no family available to assist her. She receives her cottage rent-free. And she sells the foodstuffs given to her." Mrs. Pethbridge leaned against the sofa, obviously thinking the matter settled. "I believe that's quite a bit of charity."

Not ready to release the matter, Liza asked, "Does she sell all of what we send?"

"Victoria," her mother appealed, "do you know?"

"I have only heard women discussing what she sells to the shops." She shrugged. "That is proof she doesn't need our assistance."

Liza hadn't finished her questions. "The only reason I ask is, well, if she has no coin, how does she pay for coal or wood? Or for milk? Or to replace something broken?"

The last words recalled the broken china. She didn't know what crossed her face. Clarissa was suddenly chattering about the fête, tying the conversations together by suggesting a booth to raise coins to help Mrs. Cooper and others like her. "For I know," she concluded, "that we must have others who need the occasional coins, for wood or coal or— or milk or for a treat."

"A treat? With coins donated by hard-working people?" The idea appalled the older woman, which she underlined with "I think not." She finished her tea then looked at the cart before placing her empty plate on her knee.

"A treat might be going too far," Clarissa admitted.

The idea of a booth had intrigued Victoria. "What kind of booth? We have so many. We don't have a kissing booth."

"Victoria!"

"Mama, they have a kissing booth at London fairs."

"We need not stoop to that." Mrs. Pethbridge transferred her empty china to the low table before the sofa.

"Indeed not," Liza agreed. She finished her tea and returned the cup and saucer to the lower shelf of the tea cart.

"Where would we place such a booth? When Victoria returned home yesterday, she said all the spaces were now assigned. I do agree a booth for charity is a good idea—if it does not prompt our parishioners to donate less to the alms box."

Sparky waited until the older woman leaned back then placed his forepaws on the rim of the low table. He sniffed then stretched his nose toward the plate with its crumbs of tart and cake.

Liza stood up. Sparky dropped down. Tucking his tail, he looked up at her, for he knew he wasn't permitted to eat off someone's discarded plate. She lifted him away from trouble and carried him back, whispering, "You have had quite enough."

Clarissa watched the terrier settle on Liza's lap. "We've never had a charity booth. It would be new. That alone would bring people to it. I suppose we could explain—."

"No one wants to hear a sermon, however brief, at a festival. They want to have fun. They want to buy things, gifts for other people." Victoria touched her cameo.

Keeping a hand on Sparky's collar, Liza stroked his back. "We—the booth," she amended, guessing that any suggestion that implied her ownership would nix the idea, "you would need to sell something. People who buy do not consider their purchases a contribution. And Mrs. Pethbridge is correct. We do not need to stoop to a kissing booth. That would only appeal to pock-marked young men eager to kiss pretty young ladies."

"Eww. I didn't consider that." Clarissa shuddered. "Now if it were Henry Causby—."

"And no young lady wants her husband kissing another." Victoria surprised Liza with that agreement. She leaned forward, her lovely face animated. "What if we sold tickets? A raffle?"

"That promotes gambling," her father frowned.

"Think of the possibilities, all in a good cause, Papa. We could sell chances for a—a—a picnic! Or a waltz at the fête. Or—a dozen different things, I am certain. We have only to think of them."

"None of those will work, Victoria."

"Certainly they will. A picnic with Miss Clarissa Myers. Tea with the new Mrs. Myers. A pub lunch with Mr. Myers. A waltz with me. I am certain we can enlist other young ladies."

"A pub lunch with Mr. Myers?" The vicar's eyes sparkled. "That is an idea. Quite a number of local men would like to bend his ear on issues in the village. The state of the roads in the parish. His plans to build up the local beef stock."

"A market day luncheon, here at the manor," Liza offered, "and an opportunity to explore the maze and gardens."

"Like an open day!" Clarissa clapped her hands. "Many of the great houses have them. I like that idea best, I think."

Sparky leaned forward, wanting down. She let him jump. "My husband will need to approve anything that will happen on the estate. We should not limit our scope to the vicarage and Montford. Look around the village for people with special talents. I am certain they might sell an afternoon of instruction."

"Old Mrs. Willets," Victoria exclaimed. "The one who sings at Christmas and Midsummer. I would pay for a week of lessons with her."

"Mrs. Willets has a lovely voice. Quite angelic," the vicar informed Liza.

"They say she sang Opera on the continent," Clarissa whispered. "She may have known Mozart."

Liza was impressed. "I would love to meet her."

"Have you heard of Mozart, my dear?"

Sparky returned to sit at her feet. Ears perked, eyes shining, he listened to the conversation.

"Liza is a talented pianist, Mrs. Pethbridge. What was that piece you were playing when Greville and I returned from riding?"

"Beethoven. One of his piano sonatas."

"You could make that part of the afternoon tea raffle. A piano piece by Mrs. Myers. A maze exploration. Call it 'an Amazing Afternoon with Mrs. Myers'. Ten ladies. Or twelve. Or as many as wish to come."

"Perhaps we should set a limit?"

"Now, Mrs. Myers, do not be hesitant to display your talents." The vicar polished his glasses before tucking them into a pocket. "This would be a wonderful opportunity for the ladies of the village to meet you without the dowager ruling the afternoon."

"Mr. Pethbridge," his wife hissed. "We do not call her the dowager."

Her husband remained unaffected. "That is what she is. Perhaps the dowager will admit it when we refer to her as *the dowager*. Now, Mrs. Myers, after yesterday's near misfortune, would you wish to speak with me privately? We do need to return to the village. I have my sermon to plan."

The question surprised her. "Privately?"

"In privacy, Mrs. Myers, you can share any concerns that you have. This event must have greatly distressed you."

"After my shock, I would not say *distress* was my reaction. I am extraordinarily grateful to God for sparing me." She leant down to caress the terrier's ears. He looked up and quickly licked her fingers. "Sparky saved me, you see. Would you pray, before you leave, thanking God for His great goodness? I have thanked Him, of course, yet another voice lifted in gratitude ... ."

With alacrity, he rose and came to her. Sparky watched, his tail flicking at the man who gave treats. "If you will permit, my hand on your head."

When the Pethbridges drove away, Clarissa linked their arms. "You're not escaping, you know. We must list ten ideas for the raffle tickets."

"Ten? How will you distinguish them?"

"My years of watercolor, for which I have no talent. I will paint the tickets in different colors."

"But ten ideas. Perhaps we should do five."

"Five then, unless Victoria has some brilliant ideas. I wonder how many tickets we should prepare? Come, my sister-in-law, time to put you to work on the fête."

Chapter 13

When Greville knocked on the communicating door between his bedchamber and his wife's, he expected to hear nothing. Since her arrival, he had limited himself to once-weekly visits, abstaining only when she warned him that she had her courses. The first time that occurred, she sought him in his study. With flaming cheeks, hands twisted over her heart, she gruffly said "this week is not suitable". The last time, he admitted to sadness which he convinced himself was for the lost chance of a child.

He was no longer certain of that reason.

He knocked a second time.

The oak door muffled her "Enter". Greville took a deep breath and wished his heart didn't thump in his chest. His world might change tonight, and this change felt more momentous than his marriage in April or his betrothal in January.

Clothed in white, Liza sat in the center of her bed. Her arms wrapped her drawn-up knees, with pink toes peeking from under the flannel. The bedlinens were tossed to one side, and the bed curtains pushed back, as if she had opened them when he knocked then scrambled back into place.

Yet a window curtain billowed out with the gentle night breeze. A balcony window stood open. He heard her dog snuffling around.

He'd prepared a dozen different things to say, but her wide eyes scattered them all. He wondered if he were a fool.

"Greville?" She had divined his quandary. She worried her lower lip. "The Pethbridges came today."

He knew that. He'd managed to delay his return to the manor when he counted the heads bobbing in the cart rolling along the drive. Cowardly of him to avoid the meeting, but he would have exploded if Victoria grabbed his arm, trying to claim him in front of his wife.

Liza's head tilted. "You've been volunteered for a pub lunch."

The words were so ordinary and extraordinary that it dissipated the electric charge that had seized him. "What?" exploded from him, half-laugh, half-question.

"A pub lunch, with you, as a raffle ticket for the fête."

"I'm a raffle ticket?" *Am I not hearing her correctly?*

"I'm a raffle ticket, too. An afternoon tea with Mrs. Myers. Tea. A piano recital. A walk in the maze."

He rolled his head around his shoulders but still didn't understand it. "This is for the fête?"

"It's a charity booth. To raise money to help the indigent in the parish. I didn't know you sent boxes of food to Mrs. Cooper. I think that is wonderful."

Without trying, he'd managed to impress his wife. The proof was in her awed voice and shining eyes. "Mrs. Cooper once worked on the estate."

"As a laundress, Clarissa said. She's ill. Do you think—?" Her voice trailed off, as if she wasn't certain of her idea.

"Dr. Chambers doesn't think she'll improve."

"Oh. That's sad." She bit her lip, the way he wanted to, and the electric charge powered through him again. He didn't want to pounce on her. The painting over the mantel gave him a direction to channel the energy. He planted himself before it and pretended to study the scene. A storm on the moors was all he could say, although he saw bright gold and earth-bound brown, smoky wisps, a splash of blue, and eldritch green reflecting an unseen opening in the clouds.

He jerked when Liza leaned against him. "It's a Eugenie DesChamps. *Apassionata.* I didn't intend to startle you." She paused, then in a smaller voice, she added, "I wish you had joined us for tea."

"Why did they come? Planning for the fête?" He kept his arms folded so he didn't grab her. He was ready to call off the whole festival. He didn't remember so much planning four years ago.

The terrier came and sniffed his bare feet, licked his toe, then padded to the open window.

"No. They—." She took a shaky breath.

He couldn't stop himself. He opened his arm to bring her against his side. She nestled in. Did she hear his heart thudding out of his chest?

"They heard about the urn falling. I suppose everyone's heard it. I think Mrs. Pethbridge expected me to be prostrate with hysteria. Victoria said I was cold because I only swooned."

"You're not cold. She doesn't know you."

"None of them do, not really, which is the reason I want to offer the Amazing Afternoon Tea with Mrs. Myers as a raffle."

She had manipulated him, three little strands, and he spun in her web. But he suddenly understood what she'd said earlier. "Which means I must do the pub lunch."

"Exactly. Unless—Do you not want your time to be raffled away? I know you are intensely private. You don't have to participate. Someone will pester you for an hour about things that only matter to him—."

"I'll do it, Liza."

"Oh, excellent! Clarissa thought you would."

"My sister will no doubt be delighted to prepare these events. I suppose they are her brilliant idea."

Head tilted back, her hands resting on his chest, she looked relaxed and happy. "Actually, the vicar came up with the pub lunch. I suspect he will bid for it. Victoria came up with the afternoon tea. Those were greatly preferable to the first idea. Victoria suggested a kissing booth."

Greville veered away from the thought of Liza selling kisses to men of the district. "The vicar surprises me. A pub lunch. That's a sneaky way to bend my ear. I shall have to compliment his genius on Sunday."

"I thought Victoria's idea showed genius."

"The tea and the walk in the maze will have to be delayed until we discover who pushed the urn."

She shrank visibly. Her dog whined and padded back. He rose up and braced his paws on her lower limb. She slipped from Greville's arms to pat the terrier. "It's fine, Sparky. I'm fine." He dropped down. Shivering, she wrapped her arms over her front.

"You're cold," he said. He closed the balcony door, a safer alternative to sweeping her back into his arms.

Liza stared at the painting. "Was Victoria greatly hurt, when you returned and said you were to marry me?"

She sounded curious, no more, but Greville suddenly wished he had returned for that tea rather than ducking his head and riding to a far field. He wondered into how many directions the conversation had ranged. He could not abide Mrs. Pethbridge's chatter. She had a talent for the quick snipe, which allowed Victoria to pretend to be an angel. Once he had noticed their two-part game, he soured on the local beauty. Thank God he had discovered her faults before he learned of Stanton's death.

"We weren't engaged."

"Close to engaged, your mother said. I did ask you if anyone would be hurt by our marriage."

"And I told you *no*. She might have cantered slowly toward an engagement, but I wasn't along for it."

"She's a saint to wait so long."

"I doubt it," he said bluntly, remembering clinging fingers. "She dreamed of marriage to Myers of Myers Montford. She didn't dream of marriage to me."

"Would she have married your brother, then?"

"Stanton? The golden angel who blinded all the girls? Victoria might even have grown to love him."

She looked up, her face serious, the golden shards of her wide eyes catching the firelight. "Do I have the fallen angel then?"

He stopped holding back. Once more, he wrapped his arms around her. The electric charge thrummed through him like a current that found its true line. "Fallen angel no more," and he kissed her.

.~.~.~.

Sunday, 4 September 1813

The enveloping curtains were thrown back. "Goodness!"

Greville opened a bleary eye.

Liza's maid stared, then practicality took over. "Will you be wanting coffee or tea, sir?"

"Coffee." He needed it this morning.

"I'll fetch it right away. Church this morning," she reminded. She leashed the eager terrier and led him out to a waiting footman for his morning constitutional, as Liza called it. He'd laughed at the term applied to a dog. That was his first hint of his wife's humor. She hadn't given many more clues of it after her arrival.

Liza burrowed against him. He was glad he'd taken last night's risk. He drew the covers over her shoulder before he nudged her. "Your maid is bringing your morning cuppa."

She stretched like a cat. "Where's my nightgown?"

He found it tangled in the bedcovers. She jerked it over her head as the door opened and the maid returned with a laden tray. She served her mistress first then him. He inhaled the strong aroma.

"Mercy, I thought—where is my usual cup?"

The maid folded her arms. "Broken, ma'am, like the rest of it."

"But I used it yesterday!"

"Got dropped in the washing up, ma'am. I wish I'd washed it myself, but there you are."

She looked at the tea then set the cup down. "Take this away, please."

"Now, miss—ma'am, you need your morning cuppa."

"I'll take coffee," she said firmly, "like my husband."

"He don't take sugar and cream. His valet told me. Best you start with them, ma'am."

Greville waited until the door closed again. "Broken china?" he asked, wondering if he could piece this together the way he had the raffle tickets.

He didn't expect two words to cause tears. She wiped them hastily. "I had a tea service that would serve two dozen. You remember, we would replace the chipped service with mine, but when they opened the crate, every piece was broken. And now the single set that I've used since my arrival is also broken."

China was a foolish reason to cry. He didn't understand how women attached sentiment to objects. But she shared the event because he'd asked. He leaned over and set his half-empty cup on a side table. "Sheffield is a long way for fragile freight."

"Mercy said nothing was broken when she unpacked my single service. She had to search through many of the pieces because she had to hunt for the small teapot lid. Nothing was broken then."

"Nothing was broken?" Her dark eyes glittered with unspilled tears, demanding silently that he do something. Even as he tucked her under his arm, Greville groaned inwardly. It was too early for his brain to work. Slowly he dragged the pieces into place. Liza wasn't overly sentimental. She certainly wasn't a hysteric. Her reaction after the urn proved that.

The shattered urn, the broken china. The urn deadly, the china spiteful.

"Does your maid know when the china was broken?"

"No. We thought the box room relatively secure. I would think it merely a nasty prank—."

"Except for the urn. That makes it evil. And directed at you."

"Why would anyone want to harm me?"

"Not harm. Murder. Planned. Premeditated. Evil."

She shuddered. He tightened his hold.

Her maid entered with the requested coffee, a milky brown that would hide the strong flavor. Then the woman bustled around, opening the curtains, picking up his dropped robe and draping it over the foot of the bed, all the while chattering about hot water for washing, the colors Liza would wear for today's church service. Greville watched Liza take her first sip of the coffee, close her eyes, then take a second.

"Like it?" he whispered as Mercy ran on about the cold luncheon that Cook would have for their return.

"Although that may be the amount of sugar that Mercy added."

He chuckled and reached for his robe.

"Greville, you think these two events are connected?"

"Don't you?" He planted a fist on the mattress and leaned close. "I want you to be careful. No wandering around without someone with you. Be observant. Watch for signs of trouble."

"I wouldn't have seen the urn. Sparky barked at something. I thought it was a bird."

"Sir," the maid said from the connecting door. "Rawley has a letter for you, delivered by messenger this morning."

By messenger meant a special expense. He hoped the settlements he'd invested hadn't flowed into the River Tick. "Liza, join me for breakfast?"

"Yes. I shouldn't be delayed."

"Don't be. I'm especially ravenous this morning." He bussed her mouth. Her flood of color pleased him.

.~.~.~.

Striding along the corridor, Greville passed his mother's maid hurrying with a tray. Clarissa's chamber door stood open; she was often before him. Cassandra's door remained shut.

He rapped a quick tattoo, an old habit from childhood. Hearing no response, he knocked again.

"Oh, come in, do." His younger sister sounded more than petulant.

She was dressed, perched on her bed with a large book. She wore a dyed embroidered muslin of green with yellow flowers. Without the scowl she gave him, she would have looked a pretty miss, and he told her so. Her scowl only increased.

He advanced further into the room and saw the open book was an atlas. "Planning an escape?"

"What would you care?"

"I would care very much, Sandy." He used the diminuitive from their childhood, hoping to remind her of that bond, when the four siblings had outwitted the governesses and the tutors imposed upon them by parents more often in London than at home. Stanton's return to school had been delayed, their father's attempt at economy. Though their sisters were a decade younger, the brothers helped them escape the dreary nursery and learn to love the estate.

She flipped the atlas shut and shoved it away. The bed coverings rucked under it, saving it from a crash to the floor. "So you say. But you imprison me in my room!"

Greville laughed. "Hardly a prison. You have sunshine and comfortable furnishings. I daresay Cook sent up your favorite marmalade with your breakfast."

"Don't laugh at me! You don't understand! And I don't understand *you*! You're picking *her* over us."

He sighed. His cravat felt too tight. He ran a finger under the cloth to loosen the constriction. "Back to this, Sandy?"

"Don't call me that. Why couldn't you have married Victoria?"

The question asked for all the reasons he didn't like Victoria, which he wouldn't share with a sister who couldn't control her tongue. He returned to his usual answer. "That sounds like our mother, not you.

I've explained several times the necessity of my marriage to Liza."

"She's not one of us."

"That definitely is straight from our mother. And Liza is one of us now."

"I hate her!"

"Do you?" Did she? Had she tried to kill Liza? "Do you truly hate her? Or are you parroting Mother?"

"I can think for myself. I'm not a child."

"Then don't act like one. The world does not revolve around you, Cassandra. The behavior you show me now and last night does you no credit. Mother indulges you, but I will not allow you to threaten my wife. Liza *is* my wife. That will not change. I apparently cannot expect you to overcome the prejudice our mother has instilled in you, but I do expect you to offer my wife the courtesy you have no trouble extending to others. I expect it, and I demand it."

"You don't understand."

"And you haven't attempted to understand. While we are at church, I want you to think over what I have told you, right now, last evening, and all the times I have explained our financial situation to you. Ignore what Mother has said. She chooses to remain unreasonable. Continuing in your prejudice against your sister-in-law, continuing with wild comments such as those you treated us to last night, deliberately hurting your sister with such comments, these will not endear you to any potential suitor. When you have learned basic courtesy, I will tell you the reasons that I would never have offered for Victoria. You deserve to know these things. I wish you to know them. However, as long as you continue this childish behavior, I will not. You are seventeen, Cassandra. Please show me that you are worthy of my trust."

"And if I don't? What will you do? Keep me locked in my room?"

"You are not locked in, Cassandra. I would never imprison you. This is home. But I will require you to absent yourself from company until you behave with courtesy and gratitude."

"I refuse to be grateful to *her*!"

"Think about all the ways that statement is wrong, Sandy."

He shut the door quietly. He wanted to slam it, but he couldn't expect rational behavior from Cassandra if he did not model it.

Chapter 14

At the breakfast table, Greville broke open the letter, which he discovered was from his London man of business, Mr. Vincent. Two sheets, closely written, sealed inside a third: the man certainly felt the matter was important.

The opening gave no reason for a special delivery. Vincent offered his felicitations and inquired about the members of the family, the patter that launched all his missives to Greville.

He didn't arrive at the letter's meat until two-thirds down the first page. Even then, Vincent came to his point in a roundabout manner. The Exchange stocks had vaulted in value when the French forces had abandoned Spain, with Napoleon's brother removed from that throne. Austria's entry in the coalition had steadied the stocks, which the cautious solicitor thought necessary because the French emperor had yet to face a decisive defeat. Nevertheless, Greville's investments had reaped returns that would fund the estate improvements without dipping into the principal or the quarterly payments. Corbett Mills had recently added a new business, and the returns on the old man's production remained favorable. *After years of struggles,* Vincent wrote, *Providence now smiles upon whatever you deign to touch.*

Vincent rattled out more sentences to reach the bottom of the page. Rather than turn the letter over, Greville re-read that sentence: *Providence now smiles.*

Last year's cold summer had nearly killed Montford. Other farmers had also struggled, or Greville would have caved to his solicitor's advice to sell the land. He would never have willingly turned his home over to strangers. Vincent had urged selling before major repairs became necessary. Last year, repairs to the roof, the dairy barn, the weir dam and its board-sided runs raced toward him. The mortgage ate any profits he realized. He had cursed his parents and grandparents for their profligate spending. They had escaped the consequences; he confronted them. Looking forward, he saw no possibility of a celebratory dinner with the fatted calf.

Until Mr. Vincent convinced him to sell himself through marriage to an heiress. Sinking his pride, he'd agreed before he stumbled a third time while climbing out of the pigsty.

Marriage to Liza, however, didn't make him feel like the fatted calf sacrificed for the celebrating estate. From January to April he had clawed his way out of his own class prejudice. From April to now he saw how poisonous that prejudice was.

Cassandra's words cut deepest because he had voiced them only a year before. He wouldn't permit that narrow view to re-infect him.

His mother would never bend. She might find a way to live with his decision, but she would harbor her prejudice for the rest of her life. Cassandra might cast it off if she would consider the alternative. Perhaps she thought poverty romantic because she'd never suffered an empty stomach and threadbare clothes.

Greville finished his eggs and sausages before he turned over the first page Vincent's letter to see what the man had delayed to the second page. Good news before the bad.

However, the man wrote. Greville had guessed that word was coming.

However, I have discovered distressing information about your wife. Prior to your engagement, she was romantically linked with a man named Gilbert Meaney. This man works for her grandfather. He manages a mill close to the young Mrs. Myers' home in Sheffield. Information reported to me states that Mr. Meaney visited the house several times a week. During these visits, your wife was alone with him.

Liza hadn't been with a man prior to her marriage. Greville couldn't see Vincent's purpose.

After her marriage to you, sir, your wife refused to see Mr. Meaney except for one visit on the day before she removed to Myers Montford. They met alone for a half-hour. Her mother stood outside the drawing room and refused to let anyone enter. Reports tell me that Meaney stormed out following this visit. Your wife did not appear to be in disarray although she was weeping.

The scone crumbled in his hand.

Winston appeared. "Sir? May I assist you?"

Greville tore his burning eyes from the letter. For a long second, the butler's words meant nothing. Then the question clicked, but he struggled to find an answer. "More coffee," he managed. When Winston turned away, he brushed the crumbs from his hand. He stared at the remains of the scone scattered over his plate. He picked up a portion, but his stomach revolted.

He didn't know the reason Vincent had sought information about Liza. He could see the necessity for knowing about any of her entanglements prior to their betrothal and marriage. The cogs of Vincent's machine had apparently continued to rotate slowly.

Damningly.

He didn't understand how damning until he read the next page.

It has come to my attention, sir, that in the last three weeks, Gilbert Meaney has not appeared at his place of employment by Mr. Adam Corbett. I thought nothing of that information until another informant revealed that a man of Mr. Meaney's description, calling himself Bert Manning, had found lodging in Wellesbourne Montford. I find this a strange and worrisome coincidence, sir. You are but six months' married, and I have not pressed you to make a will. I plan to arrive on Monday the Sixth, so that we can conclude that business, ensuring the safety of the estate for any future heirs of Myers blood.

.~.~.~.

Between leaving her bedchamber and arriving at the breakfast table, her husband had achieved a horrid rage. It darkened his eyes and tightened his saturnine features.

Still glowing from last night, Liza offered her sunniest smile to everyone she passed, including Clarissa and her mother-in-law when she joined them at table. Her world offered hope for their future together. Yet when she seated herself at Greville's right hand, he scowled. Her heart fell. He gave only a curt nod at her greeting and tucked a folded letter into an inner pocket.

Was that the letter that had arrived by messenger?

She hesitated to tackle Greville about his change before his mother and sister. The Myers women presented an intimidating front. Cassandra remained in exile, but both women looked unapproachable this morning. What had disturbed Clarissa's sunny mood?

Mrs. Myers was explaining that she had ordered a second carriage. "I intend to take luncheon with the Pethbridges. I did miss their company yesterday."

After a look at her brother, Clarissa opted to join her mother.

Greville delayed their departure a few minutes. The other carriage had rolled from the forecourt before they walked from the house. As always, he offered his hand as Liza climbed into the carriage. Then he chose to sit opposite her. Arms crossed, he stared out the window.

Liza waited until the coach rolled away from the house. The noisy gravel under the red wheels would hide her comments unless a groom had abnormally keen hearing.

Greville had little patience for people who ran around head-wagging, so she cut straight to the center. "What has happened? You are angry."

His lip lifted. She'd never seen his sneer. She didn't like it. "I'm not angry."

"You are treating me as if you are angry with me."

He shook his head. "Angry, Liza?" He used that silky tone from last evening. She shivered as the words slithered over her like a keen-bladed knife. "Angry isn't the correct word. I am enraged."

She waited, but he looked away and stared at the passing trees of the parkland.

Oaks bordered the drive, but maples and pines filled the understory, rampant green beyond the verge. Nothing should have captured his attention.

"Enraged at me," she ventured. Even though he gave no additional sign, she was certain. "What was in that letter? Who sent it?" When he didn't respond, she struck harder. "What lies did they tell?"

His glittering gaze pierced her. She quailed. "Who is Bert Manning?" he snarled.

She blinked. "Who?"

"Bert Manning, my dear wife."

Those words hurt. At some point, she didn't know when, she had come to yearn to be called *dear wife*. She had not wanted the words spat at her. Or with wrath growling in every syllable. She pressed against the coach seat. "I do not know that name."

His grin was predatory. "No? He has another, I understand, not so different from the alias he is using this fortnight. Do you care to guess it?"

"I wouldn't know where to start."

"Try *Gilbert Meaney*."

"Oh." That sounded weak. "I didn't tell you about him."

"No. Mr. Vincent had to do so."

So, that thin-lipped man of business had lied. Liza didn't like the man. He'd so carefully had her sign every document, so carefully explained that her husband now controlled the marriage settlements and would control every Corbett shilling when Grandfather died. She had hated Mr. Vincent on that day. *Better to hate him*, she had considered, *than the man I will marry and see every waking moment for the rest of my life. The man I've fallen in love with.*

The recognition punched through her. She gasped.

"How many secrets are you keeping, Elizabeth?"

Greville's voice rasped over raw nerves. "I did have a life before I met you," she slashed, like a wounded cat striking back.

"Gilbert Meaney is part of that old life. I did not expect him to be part of your life with me."

"He isn't."

"Don't lie, dear wife."

The words hurt just as much this second time. "I am not lying. The last time I saw Gilbert Meaney was in May, on the day before I began my journey here."

"A half-hour with him, alone, while your mother guarded the door."

"Mr. Vincent keeps spies, does he?" she snapped.

"Wisely so, *dear wife*." She hated how he underscored those words. "What did he say to you, in that half-hour? What plans did you make for your future? What vows did you make with your body?"

The questions horrified her. "No! Never. Never. He has never even kissed me."

"I do not believe you."

"I do not lie!"

"You omit the facts," he flashed.

"I told you the relevant ones," she retorted, her heat as controlled as his. "Gilbert and I were never romantically entangled. He escorted me to dances and on a few other occasions, usually at my grandfather's mandate. He never stepped over the bounds, too afraid to lose his position. At Christmas, he let me believe he was interested—then he didn't come near me again until Grandfather returned from London, and you were hard on his heels."

"Mr. Vincent says otherwise."

"Mr. Vincent listens to spies who misread the truth. Gilbert Meaney and I—no."

"Yet here he sits on our doorstep, hiding under the alias of Bert Manning."

"Show him to me," she demanded. What did card players say? She would call him out, make him ante up with the facts. "I can't believe it's the man who works for Grandfather."

"Meaney has been absent from his employment with Mr. Corbett for more than a fortnight." When she goggled at him, his frown deepened. "Prettily done, Elizabeth. I almost believe your masquerade. Unfortunately, I know your game, as does Vincent. He arrives tomorrow, to help write my will."

The turn of the carriage onto the road tilted her. Liza braced against the seat. Her Bible slipped. She clutched it, her reticule knocking against her knee. The carriage straightened onto the road, heading for the bridge, while she tried to divine what Vincent had written. In less than an hour he had turned Greville against her.

"A will? What are you talking about?"

"Without a will, since I have no issue, my wife inherits, with only token support going to my mother and sisters. My will ensures that you can't touch Myers Montford or their portions."

By some God-given grace, Liza bit her back first retort, that the manor and estate would be no great inheritance for her. It would collapse without her money, both her marriage settlements and her inheritance to come. Grandfather's will ensured that she inherited everything. Her husband would control it—a thought which made her grind her teeth every time she remembered Vincent detailing exactly how Greville would control money, property, mills, stocks, and anything else. Her second retort, also unvoiced, was that Myers Montford would be an albatross around her neck. "Do you actually think I am greedy enough to keep any part of your estate from your family? You know me not at all," she marveled.

"That's true. You hide a former lover from me."

"He wasn't my lover. And you told me nothing about your former fiancée."

"What?" His surprise was momentary. He quickly assumed that haughty mien she despised, a direct inheritance from his mother. "Victoria Pethbridge? She may have had designs on a future with me. I did not."

"That's a Banbury tale I no longer believe," she declared. "If your Mr. Vincent were here, I'd plant him the facer he deserves! He is desperate to make your will because he thinks that Gilbert Meaney and I plan to do away with you? Yes, that is what he thinks. Why else would he suggest you make a will? And rapidly, too, if he comes on the heels of this letter. He must fear you'll cock up your toes before he can arrive. That is what you think, too, isn't it?" Revolted, she could no longer look at him. "I exchanged vows with you. I shared my self with you. Yet you think—. Myers Montford is nothing more than a millstone! I would be better off with my inheritance and no man's doubts. You truly have a vile opinion of me. Stop the carriage, please." She gathered up her reticule and Bible.

"Stop the—? Why?"

Liza dashed away tears with her gloved hand. "I refuse to ride with you. I will walk into the village. There I shall purchase a ticket for the next coach that can take me back to my grandfather."

"No."

The single word ground over her, pulverizing her last dream. "You cannot tell me *no*. You forfeited that right. To think I would kill you when we—when last night—when—." A sob burst out. She pounded a fist against her knee to regain control. "Stop the carriage."

"You're not going anywhere, dear wife."

She had to wipe her eyes to see him. He blurred so quickly that she wiped them again. "You do not control me, Greville."

"Certain marriage vows give me that right."

"You think—you think I would kill you! That nullifies any bond between us." But her sob sucked the force from her words.

"You'll not go into the village while he's there. You'll not stay under the same roof as he."

Liza didn't know whether that sign of jealousy was heartening or scary. "You may be an aristocrat, but you do not rule me, dear husband." *God, is he* smiling *at me?*

"You know, dear wife, I expected you to throw that thrice-damned urn at me."

"What?"

"If you and your lover were conspiring to kill me, the urn that nearly killed you would be an excellent distraction. My death, then, would appear to be a missed attempt on you."

"That's—that's so convoluted that—I'm at sixes and sevens."

"No matter." He left his seat and joined her on the forward-facing bench.

"Please return to your side."

"No, dear wife."

She didn't—couldn't understand him. Her chest ached at his repeated use of those longed-for words. "Don't call me that," she wept, past controlling salty tears and embarrassing sobs. "Please, don't."

"You might have been happier with Gilbert Meaney," he said, confusing her further. "No obstreperous mother-in-law. No local beauty who keeps thinking she owns me. No watching your marriage settlements vanish."

She blubbered, an inelegant proof that she should never have married above her station. "I don't care about the settlements," she wailed. "Do you think all I care about is money? Do you think I would—. I-I would—. I would *never* kill you! You must think I am so cold! I would never love you then murder you!"

"I certainly wouldn't expect it after last night."

"I hate you!" she howled. When he tugged her into his arms, she wept harder. His embrace felt wonderful. She sank against him and let the tears gush.

After, she mopped her face with his handkerchief and blew her nose, more vulgarity that verified she should have never accepted his proposal. He rested his chin on her head.

"I hate crying," she whispered.

"I believe you. Since your arrival, you've had opportunities aplenty to turn into a watering pot, but you've managed to blaze through calmly."

"I haven't been calm."

"Then you should teach Cassandra how to hide her emotions. She needs lessons."

"I can't go to the church service looking like this."

"No worries, dear wife. We're almost home."

Home. She liked that word. And his *dear wife* no longer sounded hateful, but she shuddered remembering how his tone had destroyed her dream. "Don't call me that, please."

"I will call you what is the truth. You are my wife, and you are dear to me."

"I am?"

After he kissed her, awaking sparkles of pleasure, she believed him. She nestled against his silk cravat, damp from her tears. "Why do you believe me?"

"You've never cried before. Be still." He controlled her movement away. "I've seen occasional tears, but never open weeping. Never weeping that you cannot control. My mother and Cassandra have treated you horribly, and I was no help, was I? Too caught up in the estate. The constant presence of my former fiancée—."

"But you said—."

"Sh-h." He tightened his arms. "She never was, but you didn't know that. In all of that, you never wept. You sobbed now because I didn't believe you. And you have three arguments that I can't rebut, of which the chief one is that Myers Montford would be a millstone grinding you down rather than the prize Mr. Vincent considers it to be. He hasn't seen Corbett Towers. We talked of masks, Liza, didn't we? Your mask doesn't sit easily on you. Mr. Vincent will have to re-think his spies."

The carriage shook. He braced her as they turned between the gates to the estate.

In a small voice, Liza offered, "You should make any will you want. You can leave me out entirely. I don't need anything."

"Unfortunately, you will be an executor of my will. Otherwise, my mother and sisters will soon run into dun territory. Before long, the estate will be as heavily mortgaged as it was when I took over the management from my father."

"Mr. Vincent won't like that." She shut her eyes to the trees flashing past. "Mr. Vincent won't like that at all. Look what he told you, that I am trying to kill you."

"But we know differently, don't we, my love?" Liza liked that much better than *dear wife.* Several more minutes rolled past before Greville asked, "Why do you think Gilbert Meaney is here? Why do you think he is hiding under the name Bert Manning?"

Was he back to thinking she was conspiring with the man? Yet if he thought that, would he continue to hold her in his arms?

Liza tightened her fingers, gripping his torso. "That last time I saw him, he said that I would soon hate my life with an uppity gentleman like you. He said no one would accept me." *Gilbert was very nearly right,* she admitted silently. Only Clarissa had accepted her. Greville had made use of her, but somewhere, somehow that had transformed. The falling urn had brought the change to his attention.

Without the urn, would Mr. Vincent's letter have killed any blossoming affection between them?

Chapter 15

"Whose dogcart is that?" Liza tucked her hand in Greville's to steady her descent from the carriage.

"The vicar's."

"He should be at the church, for the service."

His mother would have sailed past, blithely ignoring the piebald horse and cart standing just past the entrance, untended by footman or groom. Liza had marked it as soon as he had. That gave him another reason to consider her an excellent match, even though he'd taken months to apprehend it.

No footman appeared at the great door to admit them.

"Where's Winston?"

"He'll have gone to the service with the other servants." He thought she knew the house staff rode wagons into the village on Sundays and market days.

"Yes, I know that, but on Sunday every servant doesn't go. I thought a footman and a couple of maids stayed here, taking it in turns."

Greville opened the massive door then stood back to let Liza precede him. She smiled up at him. Her eyes still looked puffy.

Drawing off her gloves, she walked slowly to the round table that centered the entrance. Then she cried out and rushed to the stairs.

When he saw a woman crouched at the foot of the stairs, bending over something on the floor, he called back to the carriage "Wait!" Then he hastened after Liza.

She stopped abruptly then fell to her knees beside the woman. Her reticule and Bible dropped to the floor as she reached for the body lying there.

"No! Don't!" The crouching woman pushed her away. She looked around, and Greville recognized Victoria. "Thank God you have come. I didn't know what to do."

"It's Cassandra." Liza flung off her remaining glove.

His sister looked like a broken doll, crimson skirts spilled around her still body Like the flowers in the urn that had nearly killed Liza. Mercifully unconscious, Cassandra was not screaming in pain from her broken arm. She had landed awkwardly, with her other arm flung out and a leg bent under her. How had she fallen?

What if she hadn't fallen?

Greville jerked, a marionette readied for a performance by a puppetmaster.

"She breathes! She breathes, Greville." That was Liza, bringing him out of his trance as she ran her hands along his sister's limbs and shoulders. "Send for the doctor."

"Yes. Yes! I didn't know what to do." Victoria's famed serenity had abandoned her.

"Cor!" came a voice behind him. "It be a lady down."

Greville swiveled around and jabbed a finger at the groom. "Ride fast for Dr. Chambers. Tell him my sister has fallen down the stairs. She is unconscious. Make haste, man."

The youth stopped goggling and ran out the door.

"Should I carry her to a sofa?" he asked when Liza sat back on her heels.

"We should not move her, not until the doctor permits." Her gaze climbed the long flight to the first floor. "If she fell all the way—."

"She could have internal injuries," he finished when she would not.

"We should cover her. The floor is cold. There's a rug in the large sitting room. Victoria, would you—?"

Victoria scrambled to her feet. Mute, she brushed past Greville without acknowledging him.

He studied his sister's colorless face, her flickering eyelids, the pale blonde hair spilled around her, stark contrast to the crimson gown. "She's so pale."

Liza touched Cassandra's cheek. Her lashes fluttered. She moaned. "Cassandra," she whispered, "wake up, wake up."

He knelt to add his voice and touch. "Sandy, wake up." He touched her out-flung hand, but she only whimpered.

"I found this." Victoria draped the rug over Cassandra, tucking it up to her chin.

"Have you seen any of the servants?" Liza asked Victoria.

"What do servants matter? Cassandra could be dying, and you need servants?"

His wife's mask shuttered down, defense against people who didn't understand her. She didn't snap at Victoria, merely explained tonelessly, "A room should be readied for her. I do not think Dr. Chambers will want her carried up all those steps. Perhaps the small sitting room? I need to find whoever is here."

"Do whatever you think is best," Greville said. When she started to rise, he sprang to assist her. "My dependence is on you."

Her mask cracked. He received a tender look, then she hurried past the stairs to the long hallway bisecting the manor, for there was the green baize door that led to Belowstairs. He watched until Liza turned into the hall then looked back at his sister.

Cassandra had escaped from pain by slipping back into unconsciousness. He feared that unnatural sleep, but for her sake, he hoped she remained in it until the doctor with his medicines arrived.

Cassandra had defied him. As soon as the family and most of the servants left the house, she escaped her exile. And she'd stolen clothes from Liza.

He recognized that crimson gown, with its black ribbons on the bodice and sleeves and white ruffling lace around the scooped neckline and twirling hem. Liza had worn it to the Midsummer Ball hosted by the Davenports. He stared at the lacy ruffle with its black stitchery and remembered how his wife's jet earrings had danced as he whirled her around in the scandalous waltz. He'd seen no other gown like it that evening.

Cassandra had complained the whole drive to and from the Davenports. She didn't understand the reason debutantes wore white. She had demanded a red gown of her own, "as soon as we're in London, Mama," at which point his mother criticized the gown as too flamboyant, too bourgeois.

He'd buy his sister a dozen red gowns if she survived this without great hurt.

But why had she taken Liza's gown?

His brain hung on that question.

He couldn't get past the belief that Cassandra hadn't fallen. Cassandra, in Liza's gown, lying at his feet. Cassandra, injured because she wore Liza's gown. Had someone seen the highly recognizable gown and pushed Cassandra down the stairs? Mistaking Cassandra for Liza. Wanting to harm Liza. That was the only answer.

"Waiting is the hardest." Victoria interrupted his thoughts.

Greville paced back from the marble-topped round table with its vase of the last Portland roses. He stopped once more beside Cassandra's limp body, but he studied Victoria, wondering what had brought her to Montford when the whole house had headed to the church service her father conducted.

She hadn't removed her summer straw bonnet with its green ribbon that matched her pelisse. She still wore her kid gloves.

Liza's gloves lay on the floor, dropped carelessly beside her embroidered purse and Bible. Her silly shepherdess bonnet likely still lay on the floor of the carriage, where he'd dropped it when the brim interfered with their kissing. Victoria's bonnet framed her classically pure features, which had never inspired him to steal a kiss. Her earlier anxiety was vanished, replaced by her serene mask. *Can I shake that serenity enough to find the truth she is always careful to step around?*

"You would know waiting is hard."

She flinched at his deliberate cruelty, but she didn't retreat. "Yes. Four years. Three years too long."

"Your choice. I never gave any promises."

Her green eyes narrowed. Her visible control amazed him. "Your mother swore—. My mistake. I listened to what I wanted to hear, not to what you were saying. When your brother was found dead, I did expect your courtship. Your mother suggested that was the reason you had waited."

"Her expectations, not mine. Your decision to wait, not mine. You wanted to be Mrs. Myers, not my wife."

"A fine distinction," she sneered.

"A true one. I understood it, as I understand that if Stanton had returned, you would have transferred your attentions to him. Your heart wasn't engaged, only your greed. And you're still not listening to me, or you wouldn't come here four days of every week."

"I—my apologies. I was not aware that my presence created difficulties for—for you."

He couldn't let those words stand, for they insinuated that she affected him in some way. "You don't affect me. Nor my wife." He underscored the last word. "You are creating difficulties for my mother, however."

"For your mother?"

He'd surprised her. Victoria lifted a hand to him, expecting his assistance. Greville kept his hands clasped behind him. Her face colored bright red, an unbecoming shade for a blonde. Her fist clenched. Her hand dropped. She remained kneeling.

"How do I create difficulties for your mother?"

"You don't know? Perhaps I know you better than you know yourself, Victoria. I doubt a single week can pass without a cutting comment from you about Liza. Or how money can buy everything except true hearts. Or how Liza's suggestions about the manor will change it into a middle-class monstrosity. Have I missed anything recent?"

"I never—."

"I heard that last one, Victoria. Don't lie."

From bright red she went paler than Cassandra. "Your mother doesn't want her home changed."

"The drawing room curtains are rotting on their hooks," he countered.

"You don't understand. You are only concerned with the land. This house is your mother's home."

"And mine. And now Liza's."

She scrambled to her feet, clumsy without help. "I never expected you to treat me this way!"

"How? By telling you the truth?" He remembered Cassandra's call for the truth. "How do I hurt you with the truth?"

Rapid footsteps came running, halting their argument.

A maid ran from the hall. She skidded when she saw Cassandra. Her hands flew to her mouth, as if she would vomit. Then she dashed away, turning in the direction of the smaller sitting room. More footsteps. A footman passed along the hall. Mrs. Grunby came, accompanying his wife.

"—easy enough to put up, ma'am," the housekeeper said. "I think that iron bedstead will work fine."

"I am so thankful you are here. I would have had no idea what could be utilized. Miss Cassandra will likely be convalescent for weeks."

"We'll soon have the room to rights, Mrs. Myers." The housekeeper stopped at the foot of the stairs. "Poor young thing."

Liza clasped her hands together on her bosom. "Has she roused? No? That lack of consciousness worries me."

Mrs. Grunby murmured to his wife then retreated while Liza knelt beside her sister-in-law. "She looks so fragile. Like a china doll."

"She has on your dress," he said harshly.

"She does? Oh, I didn't notice. Yes, I wore that at Midsummer."

Victoria stirred. "I should leave. I am only in the way."

Greville laughed. "Have you decided you no longer want to live in my mother's pocket? Why *are* you here? You never miss your father's sermons."

"I—I needed something."

"Come, Victoria. Be more specific. What brings you here, when the house is relatively empty, just when my sister falls down the stairs? While wearing my wife's dress?"

Liza shot him a look. Then she paled. She started up. He quickly assisted her and kept her close to his side.

"I came—. Your mother—."

"Do not be reticent. Tell us." When she delayed, he growled, "Did you think it was Liza that you pushed down the stairs?"

"I didn't."

"Greville—."

"No, I didn't," Victoria insisted. "I tried to help Cassandra."

"You helped her all the way down the stairs?"

"No! You are mad to think this!"

"Yes, I am, when someone attacks my sister. When they try to murder her, just as they tried to murder my wife."

"Greville, I don't think that now——."

"How dare you accuse me! I would *never* harm Cassandra."

He waited until the entrance no longer echoed with her shriek. "But you would harm Liza? That's true, isn't it?"

His wife stopped tugging his arm and turned her shocked gaze on serene Victoria Pethbridge, serene no more.

"You are the one that put the idea in Cassandra's head that it would be better if the urn hadn't missed."

"I said that in jest!"

"No one jokes about murder, Victoria. Did you see that red dress with its black ribbons? There's not another like it in the district. Isn't that what you said at Midsummer—but not as a compliment, was it? Did you see the dress and follow it down the hall? Did you think *one little push*?"

"I would never hurt anyone!"

"One little push, and she's gone. One little push, and he has the money and still needs the wife."

Distaste warped her face. "I cannot believe I ever thought you worthy of me. I am leaving!"

"Not yet, Victoria. Not until you tell me the reason you came this morning and the reason you hadn't sent for help."

"I hadn't had time. I had just arrived and found her."

"Tell a better lie. Your horse has been standing a while."

"You are insufferable!"

"You have to answer, Victoria. Have you forgotten that I'm magistrate of this district?"

She fumed, fists clenched at her sides, feet stomping on the floor, stomping the hem of the red dress. "I hate you," and she cursed him, using words he would never have expected a vicar's daughter to know.

Cassandra whimpered, silencing Victoria. Liza dropped beside her. She tucked the rug closer. "Dr. Chambers is coming. Your brother is here. All will be well. Soon, my pet, soon."

She lapsed again although this time her brow remained furrowed.

"I didn't hurt her," Victoria said quietly, a forced calm that didn't touch the anger that ruined her beauty. "And I would not hurt your wife. I did say—that. It was wrong of me, but I thought you—wanted me. I have believed other people when I should not. I should have listened to you. You were—clear."

"The reason you're here?"

"You'll find it, soon enough." She sounded exhausted. Her slumped shoulders and bent head exhibited defeat. "I left a letter for you. A foolish dream. Burn it, please, instead of opening it. If you have even an iota of loyalty to my father—I don't expect you to have any for me. But the letter—. I thought you were trapped, you see. I flattered myself with my little dream. Please burn that letter."

"And Cassandra?"

Her head came up. "I didn't go upstairs. I didn't! I went to your study. I was there when—when I heard her fall. I found her, just like this, only two or three minutes before you arrived. I didn't know what to do."

What could she have been doing in his study? Dreaming of him as her husband, sitting in his chair, behind his desk, touching his quills and blotter.

"Greville, I believe her." Liza's arm slipped around the back of his waist. He hadn't seen her rise; she just suddenly offered comfort.

He believed that sorry little story, too. But he dared not risk it was a lie. "I have no evidence. Without evidence, I will not accuse. When Cassandra wakes, we'll ask what she remembers."

"She won't remember me. I wasn't the one."

That calm insistence was more believable than her earlier vehemence. "Even so," he told her, "I will look for evidence. I thank you for the truth that you *have* told, Victoria."

She paled. "I will leave now, if I may. If you decide that I am guilty, I am easily found. My father—my father will come and pray for Cassandra. If you wish him to do so."

He couldn't answer. He couldn't reconcile the woman who wished Liza were dead with the woman who recommended that most sacred of Christian offerings to God.

"Victoria?"

She stopped so quickly that he knew she still hoped, a foolish dream that his next words would crush. She didn't turn. Her swan's neck supported her bent head.

"My mother has depended greatly on you, for the management of this house and her charities and the fête. I know she is most appreciative. Nevertheless, I would prefer that you not come to the house or the estate without the escort of your father."

Without comment, she nodded then walked out, past the round table, through the massive opening, for the door stood wide, awaiting the doctor's arrival.

He tightened his embracing arm around Liza, as if he could meld her to him. "You have to be careful," he warned her. Her nod wasn't enough. "Listen to me, Liza. You *have* to be *careful*. This wasn't an accident."

She didn't answer.

They could hear the servants in the long hall, talking as they carted in what they needed to transform the sitting room into a convalescent's room, one that he prayed Cassandra would need.

Liza stirred. "She was here that day, you know. When the urn fell."

He hadn't forgotten. "It's doubly damning that she found Cassandra."

"She wouldn't hurt your sister, Greville."

"That's the problem, Liza. Cassandra wore your gown. Whoever pushed her thought that they pushed you."

Chapter 16

Rolling down his shirt sleeves, Dr. Chambers emerged from the converted sitting room.

Greville whirled around and strode back down the long hall to speak with the physician. Cassandra's whimpering came into the hall before the door shut. Those wounded sounds hurt him more than her first screams on waking.

He expected his mother and Clarissa momentarily. The second groom, sent to the church to inform his mother and sister, had not yet returned. If he'd had his wits, he would have asked the first groom to notify them after he found Dr. Chambers. A mistake, one that Victoria must not have rectified when she arrived in the village. The ticking clock reminded him that time passed, but when he looked at the round dial with its painted sun, only a scant two hours had passed since he and Liza had returned home.

Dr. Chambers shrugged into the jacket that the footman held for him. "I've sedated her. She'll be in pain for quite some time. Broken arm, collar bone, leg. I've stabilized the breaks with splints and wraps. Quite a knot on her head. Your wife promises to keep close watch. I do not want your sister drifting off for the next few hours. Head injuries are dangerous."

"What should I do?"

"Not much you can do. Keep her comfortable. Not too much laudanum, mind. If her brain were not injured, I would not worry about deep sleeping. As it is—. She's young, healthy. Broken limbs properly set will knit back. The head, now, that's tricky business."

"My mother will be greatly distressed."

Dr. Chambers' level look revealed that he knew Amabel Myers' version of distress. "Miss Clarissa Myers is reasonable. She can look after her mother. You didn't say how Miss Cassandra came to fall."

"We don't really know."

"Your wife said much the same. She informed me that Miss Pethbridge was present?"

"She claims to have found Cassandra."

The doctor pursed his lips. "No evidence, I surmise? Servants not about?"

"Most attended the church service. The others were Belowstairs."

"I saw Miss Pethbridge on Friday. In passing."

"I'm aware, doctor."

Dr. Chambers' eyes narrowed. Greville might have shared whole pages of speculation, but he left them unsaid. He would not accuse Victoria without evidence. She was the vicar's daughter, well regarded in the community. Since her ambitions were rarely thwarted, few people had encountered the ruinous acid she dripped from concealed fangs.

"I will return this evening, Mr. Myers. Your wife promises to stay with your sister. I will bring with me a nurse for the night hours. Clarissa—once she's dealt with the elder Mrs. Myers, can spell your wife in the day until I find a second nurse. By tomorrow evening, we will have a better grasp of what the knock to her head has done to her brain. She will be convalescent several weeks, knitting those bones back."

.~.~.~.

When he'd seen the doctor off, Greville returned and eased into the sitting room.

Liza turned from her station at the four-poster bed. She remained mute as he came to the bedside.

Cassandra was as white as the bedlinens. The narrow bed had been set up to receive the afternoon light. The sweep of her lashes formed pale fans on her cheeks. With her hair loose across the pillows and her mouth opened, she looked like a little girl innocently asleep. That image was wrecked by the bulky splint on her forearm, the wrappings that immobilized her shoulder, and the cumbersome splint on her lower limb, hidden by a light sheet.

Greville's anger lifted its predatory head, sniffing for prey—but he had no one as its focus.

"Her breathing's labored," he murmured.

Liza slipped her fingers into his. "Dr. Chambers expects that. She is in pain."

"Can she hear us?"

"I think. He gave her laudanum. He doesn't want to her to sleep very deeply, though."

"Has she spoken?"

"Not of her fall."

"His suspicions match ours."

She frowned and tweaked a corner of the sheet. "I said nothing."

"Nor did I, but he's an intelligent man. He can put the pieces together. Coupled with the urn, with Cassandra wearing a dress that people associate with you, it's very suspicious."

The door opened. "Sir?"

Winston had returned, which meant the other servants had also returned from the village. His mother and Clarissa would soon follow.

"A moment, Winston. Liza, did the doctor have a suggestion for treatment of my mother? She will be devastated with grief."

"He suggested no more than ten drops of laudanum."

"See that Clarissa has them available when she needs them for our mother." He briefly tightened his clasp then went to deal with the butler.

Winston stood at his study door. "Is Miss Cassandra going to recover, sir?"

"The doctor believes so. He recommends extreme quiet for the next few days."

"Mrs. Grunby informed us, sir, of the circumstances of Miss Cassandra's fall. She found no sign of intruders. Potts is searching the grounds. Whoever is doing this evil, sir, they must be stopped. First Mrs. Myers. Now your sister. The next person attacked could be killed."

"Did Mrs. Grunby account for all of the servants?"

"She accounted for every person who remained here as well as those who returned with me when Jamie brought the word. Jamie remained to inform the dowager, sir."

How easily Winston had fallen into the new title for his mother. One thing going right in a world all hurly-burly.

"The service had reached the prayers," Winston continued.

Which meant only a few more minutes of grace remained. "Did you see Miss Pethbridge's dogcart?"

"Yes, sir. I thought it odd that she missed service. Had she come here?"

"She found my sister."

"Did she now? Mrs. Grunby did say that Miss Cassandra was wearing your wife's ball gown from Midsummer." Imitating Dr. Chambers, Winston pursed his lips rather than share his thoughts. "Your man-of-business Mr. Vincent has arrived, sir. He waits in your study for a private conference."

Greville started. "Vincent has arrived?"

"Mrs. Grunby is preparing a room for him, sir, as he expects to conduct business with you on the morrow." All of his news given, Winston opened the study door and stepped back.

"Bring me word of what Potts discovers."

"Sir," and when Greville had entered, the butler closed the study door.

His man of business turned from contemplating a landscape over the mantel, a green and gold painting of the willow pond in late summer. Aged by the stress of his work, his pale face was lined by worry, but the steel-grey eyes peering over his pince-nez were keenly observant. Narrow of face, lean of body, he wore an old-fashioned frock coat of superfine. His stockings and polished shoes also pre-century. In one hand he gripped a slender envelope case which he tapped against his leg. "At last. Sir. How is Miss Cassandra? I was informed of her injuries upon my arrival."

Once again, Greville repeated the doctor's hopes. "She has weeks of convalescence before her. She will not be an easy patient, that I can guarantee. I expected you tomorrow, Vincent."

His small mouth twisted. "Once I franked my letter for the post, I had worries about any delay. I regret that my worries were founded."

"Just not in the direction you anticipated."

Vincent's hand cut down. "We shall see, sir. I never expected her vile plan to focus upon your family. We shall have to guard against—."

Remembering the contents of Vincent's letter, Greville tried to stop the incipient accusations. "Mr. Vincent, you should not believe that my wife Liza injured my sister Cassandra?"

"Indeed, Mr. Myers. I know you are reluctant—."

"Liza was with me, in the carriage, when Cassandra was pushed down the stairs."

"Was she?"

"I see you do not believe me. Tell me, Vincent, if I had not needed to wed an heiress, who would you have considered a suitable bride for me?"

The subject change flustered the man. "Sir, this has nothing to do—."

He was too tired, too angry, and too frustrated to allow the solicitor to flail in false waters. "Did you think that I would offer for Miss Victoria Pethbridge?"

"A virtuous young lady of that sort—."

"I understand how few opportunities you have had to receive a proper reading of Victoria Pethbridge's personality. I will tell you this, Vincent. I suspect that Victoria pushed Cassandra down the stairs. She claims to have found her. I find it suspicious that she comes to the house when only Cassandra and a few servants are here. I find it doubly suspicious that she had not called for help when she found Cassandra. I question how long she would have left my sister lying on the cold floor."

"Sir, Miss Pethbridge would have no reason to attack Miss

Cassandra."

"True. Cassandra, however, had raided my wife's closet. She wore a gown easily recognizable as belonging to my wife. Whoever pushed Cassandra must have mistaken her for my wife. That, Vincent, means that Cassandra was not the intended victim of this malicious act. My wife was. And I will accept from you no more accusations against Liza."

Vincent sank onto the sofa and blinked. He removed his pince-nez, stared at them as if he didn't understand how they came to be in his hand, then replaced them on his nose. "Sir, what reason—? Miss Pethbridge is the daughter of your vicar. She has a sweet disposition—."

"As I said, very clearly, you have had no opportunity for an accurate reading Victoria Pethbridge. She is not the sweet gentlewoman that most believe."

"Sir, I do not believe—if you have been poisoned against her—."

"Poison. That is an accurate description. I have been poisoned against her, *by* her, long before I discovered that I needed to marry to save this estate. Please be aware that Victoria has also poisoned Cassandra herself and my mother against Liza. Clarissa is not so easily influenced, thank God. Victoria wanted to turn my family against Liza."

"Sir, I have difficulty—."

Greville held up a hand to stop Vincent's counter. "You were not at dinner with us last evening. A very uncomfortable dinner, Vincent. Cassandra treated us to a tantrum, of which one part was her wish that Liza were dead. This is evidence of Victoria's manipulation of my younger sister."

"Sir, if the new Mrs. Myers has alienated your family—."

"It's more that my family wishes to alienate my wife *from* me. Miss Pethbridge encourages them. Spite. I will allow you to surmise the reason."

The wizened man gaped as his mind sifted through Greville's evidence. Then he looked at the portfolio clutched in his bone-white fingers. "I brought the verification my people have accumulated."

"Of a false relationship between Liza and this Gilbert Meaney. She has explained that to my satisfaction."

"Women can have winning ways, sir, such wily charms that a man forgets good sense."

"Shall I say it bluntly, then? You've grabbed the wrong end of the stick, Vincent. Let me apprise you of a recent circumstance that changes everything. Liza was nearly killed on Friday. Someone pushed off one of the roof urns. It nearly struck her."

"A roof urn? I saw them missing. But if you have mistaken an accident for——."

"Not an accident. The urn had clearly been shifted earlier. Talk to Mr. Potts. He spotted it before I did. In light of that obvious attack on my wife, what do you now think of Cassandra's fall down the stairs, especially as she was clearly mistaken for my wife?"

"I do not know what to think."

"Then I will give you one more piece of evidence. The attack on my wife was premeditated, for the urn was shifted several days previous. Someone wants my wife dead."

He dropped the portfolio onto his bony knees.

"I believe that you owe my wife an apology, Vincent."

"I may have misjudged the situation somewhat," he allowed, ever cautious.

"You misjudged it completely. As you have misjudged my wife, operating under the same class prejudice that rules my mother, which Victoria Pethbridge used to manipulate her. Someone has made two attempts to kill my wife. I do not wish a third attempt to succeed. Bend your mind to that problem, Vincent, and drop this foolish conspiracy involving her and Gilbert Meaney."

His head lifted. His thin nostrils looked pinched. "That man is here, sir, in Wellesbourne Montford. Your pub host told me as much when I stopped for refreshment before coming here. He has disguised himself as Bert Manning. Why would a man present himself under a false name unless he has a nefarious purpose? He's waiting for someone, the host said."

"My wife is not conspiring with Gilbert Meaney. Remove that from your head and take a fresh look at your so-called evidence with Liza as the victim of these two attacks."

Women's agitated voices interrupted him. Greville turned to deal with them. "I can give you no more time at present, Vincent. My mother and sister have returned. I suggest you retire to the chamber Mrs. Grunby has prepared."

"Sir, this evidence——."

"Drop it, Vincent. Burn it, for all I care. Good Lord, if you want a good reading on my wife, ask Winston and Mrs. Grunby. Ask any of the servant who interact with her. They don't hesitate to follow her orders. That's never been the case with my mother." He strode from the room.

. ~ . ~ . ~ .

Voices sharp and strident filled the hall. The murmured response must be Liza or Clarissa. "I will not have you anywhere near her!" his mother shrieked.

"Please!"

That was Cassandra's cry.

He reached the open doorway. His mother stood on one side of the bedstead, jabbing a finger at Liza on the other side. Third in the triangle around Cassandra, Clarissa wrung her hands.

The afternoon sun cast its light on the windows, creating a glare that obscured the last flowers in the brick planters of the terrace and the boxwoods that formed the maze. The light filled the room, removing all shadows, illuminating the faces of the four women. Cassandra looked wan, but she had awakened, giving him hope for her recovery. Liza had crossed her arms as she watched Cassandra. His mother and Clarissa glared at each other, so alike yet so different.

"Go away," his little sister appealed.

"I will not have *her* looking after my angel!"

"Sh-h," Liza entreated. "Cassandra needs rest. Dr. Chambers asked for quiet."

"I want you gone! Out of my house. You probably pushed her."

"No—," Cassandra whimpered.

"Mama, we should not discuss this here."

Still angry at Vincent, Greville fumed at this second false accusation against his wife. "Liza was with me," he gritted. "Cassandra fell while we were gone. Victoria was with her when we arrived."

"Victoria! My Victoria?" From astonishment Mrs. Myers snapped to anger. "Then *she* must have set a trap that my angel fell into."

"That's not possible, Mother, and you know it. You were last down the stairs before we left for church. Unless that trap was of your own making."

"I did no such thing!"

"Go 'way."

"Sandy, how did you fall?"

Her eyes squeezed shut. "Didn't."

"You fell to the bottom of the stairs," he explained, thinking she didn't understand his question. "Victoria found you. We were all gone to church. You crept from your room. You took Liza's Midsummer gown, remember?"

"What are you saying?" his mother demanded. "She was wearing *her* gown? This is *her* fault."

"I don't think Liza lent her gown to Cassandra, Mama. Cassandra likely took it, the way she takes my clothes that she likes when no one's around to stop her."

"Red."

He hung over her bed. "Yes, Cassandra. You wore Liza's red gown."

She whimpered. "Hurts."

"The doctor said I could give her more laudanum."

"No! You will not poison my daughter."

But Liza looked only to Greville for permission. When he nodded, she immediately turned to obey. The dark opiate bottle stood on a side table, with a child's silver beaker, a blue-tinted glass, and a pitcher. He braced a hand on the iron crossbar of the headboard. "Cassandra? Did you trip? You fell all the way."

"Pushed," she whispered.

"It should have been *her*. She's brought nothing but harm to this family."

Liza returned with the silver beaker. "Drink this, Cassandra."

"No."

"It will ease the pain. Dr. Chambers said so."

Disputes were suspended as Liza carefully lifted the young woman's head so she could drink. She moaned, and his mother whirled away from the bed. She drew out a lacy handkerchief and dabbed her eyes.

"One more sip," Liza coaxed. When Cassandra's head returned to her pillow, sweat had beaded on her forehead.

"Sandy," Greville insisted, hoping to settle the chief question.

"She needs quiet," Liza reminded. "She is not to sleep, but she doesn't need to be disturbed with this. Surely your questions—your accusations can wait or be conducted elsewhere."

"All but one question. Sandy, listen to me."

Her lashes fluttered.

"Greville," his mother cautioned.

"Sandy, did you fall?"

Her head moved slightly, then she whimpered. "Pushed. Go `way, all of you."

Greville straightened. He caught his mother's eye and gestured to the door.

"I will *not* leave! She is my daughter. I should take care of her."

"When you can do so calmly, you may. For now, we should give Cassandra the quiet she needs. Liza will stay."

Yet the butler appeared in the still-open door. "Sir. Mrs. Myers has a guest. A lady who claims that she is her mother."

"My mother has been dead this score of years."

Winston didn't falter. "The young Mrs. Myers. She gives *Mrs. Seth Corbett* as her name. She has an escort, ma'am. Mr. Gilbert Meaney."

The man who had pretended to court his wife.

Liza blanched. Her color was slow to return. He was inordinately pleased when she turned to him. "I cannot leave Cassandra."

"Clarissa."

His sister didn't hesitate. "Of course, Grev. What must I do, Liza?"

"Give her water when she asks. From the silver cup. It will seem cooler. You can wet her lips and sponge her face. The cloth and basin are there. Talk quietly. Try not to bump the bed. Oh, if she seems in great pain," and she repeated the doctor's instructions about the laudanum.

"Mother, if you will come with me. We need to talk."

"Is my son going to exile me from this room?"

"Shall we discuss options?"

Liza finished her whispered conversation with Clarissa. She preceded them to the hall and delayed only to ensure Winston left the door open. "For it draws the air and keeps her cool." Then she stopped, clearly perplexed. She reached a hand to Greville.

He snared it and pressed it between both of his. "Do you wish me to accompany you?"

Her gaze flicked to his mother and back. "Husband, will you join us in a few minutes?"

He touched her cheek. "Explain to them the events of the past days, Liza. That should keep their attention until I arrive."

His mother took issue with those promised few minutes. "My concerns will not be dismissed in a *few* minutes, Greville. You are much mistaken if you think they will be."

Liza shook out her skirts then lifted her chin high. "Where did you put these visitors, Winston?"

"Your sitting room, ma'am." He sniffed, a clear indication that he didn't think them worthy of the drawing room, not until Mrs. Corbett's identity was confirmed.

"Lord, what a tangled web this is," Liza muttered, almost like a prayer.

"Mother, shall we use my study?" He could only hope that Mr. Vincent had vacated it. He didn't want those two conferring until the lawyer straightened out his evidence.

Chapter 17

Liza convinced Winston that she could let herself into the sitting room while he conveyed to Cook that two more might attend the late luncheon. "Might," she emphasized. After that emotionally wrought carriage ride with Greville, she was not certain she ever wanted to see Gilbert Meaney again.

Winston sniffed again. "Shall I have service in the half-hour, ma'am?"

"Shall we see how this conversation advances? Do have something taken to Miss Clarissa. She may be closeted with Miss Cassandra for some time."

"Very good, ma'am. I will have James or John stand without this door."

"Excellent." Liza placed her hand on the doorknob as the butler headed on. *Seeing Mother should not give me any anxiety. I did wish her to come. Just not now.*

She had no desire to see Gilbert. Only a couple of hours before had Greville revealed Mr. Vincent's accusations of a convoluted conspiracy. Gilbert had nothing to do with those accusations, but she was hesitant to have any exchange with him. He wasn't the agent of those accusations. She shouldn't consider him a culprit.

When she considered Greville's difficult meeting with his mother, she cringed. Encountering Gilbert was nothing to that meeting. Her husband had her sympathies, for his mother was often unreasonable. Yet she should not continue to blindly accuse Liza of misdeeds. *When did her dislike explode into such antipathy?*

The shattered urn had broken the façade of mere dislike.

Had Mrs. Myers planned to rid herself of a despised daughter-in-law?

My death would free Greville to marry a woman of their station.

The admission pained her, but she had to accept it—and then wonder if the dowager had ordered one of the gardeners to shift the urn a few inches. Had she then sent Cassandra or Victoria to complete the plan with a mere push? Fed by the double poison of her mother and Victoria, would Cassandra have hesitated? Victoria's motivation was her potential marriage to Greville. Or was Clarissa the other side of the plot? Clarissa, who disguised hatred with a friendly mask?

If she speculated much longer, she would become paranoid.

Whoever drove the master plan, today it had gone horribly wrong. *We delayed our departure this morning. Did Mrs. Myers think I would not attend the service? Did she send Victoria for a second attempt?* Victoria must have recognized Liza's Midsummer gown, worn again on Saturday evening. She had seized her chance only to be appalled when she discovered Cassandra at the foot of the stairs.

If Victoria was the culprit?

Who else could hate her so much?

"Ma'am?"

A footman stood behind her, arriving while she tried to work out the connection between the two attempts at murder.

For murder was the intention, she had no doubt.

"Did Winston give you any orders?"

"To stand ready if you need me, ma'am."

"I depend on you."

He nodded. Reaching past her, he turned the knob she had released during her stress-filled ponderings. Pressing a hand over her racing heart, Liza entered the sitting room.

Standing by Liza's desk was woman in a military-braided pelisse of Pomona green. Her gloved hands, with a similar black braiding on the cuffs, sifted through the papers on the blotter. She turned her head, and the curved ostrich feathers of her bonnet brushed her cheek. Deborah Corbett retained the beauty that had attracted Adam Corbett's son. In her daughter, that pure line of straight nose and pert chin were flattened by the father's stamp.

Unconcerned at being caught snooping, she turned to greet her daughter. "Liza. You look a little flushed. Do you have a sickness?"

"No, Mother, I do not." She extended her hands to greet her mother, and they brushed cheeks. "That's a lovely hat. New?"

"Of course. When Mr. Meaney proposed this journey, I simply had to have a new ensemble for traveling. Do you like it?" She touched the brim of her bonnet, also festooned with black braiding.

"Where is Mr. Meaney? The butler announced you both."

"He wished to explore the maze. He will return in a few minutes, I am certain."

"If Mr. Meaney can discover the way out of the maze."

"Is it a puzzle maze then? I thought it a walk."

"It's not a puzzle if you know the trick. Left and left then right and—."

"Goodness, it's no use telling me. I will not be wandering it."

No, Deborah Corbett never ventured into gardens or on long walks.

Blessed with a trim figure, she retained it with strict diet. She lowered herself to the chintz-covered settee with its abstracted florals. One gloved hand rested on the curved arm. The other lay relaxed in her lap. "I was beginning to think you were lost somewhere in this house, and that man had difficulty locating you."

"Winston knew where I was. We've had an upset this morning." She was diminishing the severity of Cassandra's fall, but how should she describe the event with the drama it deserved without sounding hysterical?

"The man said that one of the daughters of the house fell on the stairs. Which one, dear?" She slowly withdrew her gloves, revealing glittering rings, for Deborah Corbett liked to display the wealth she'd married. No doubt when she removed the traveling pelisse, two or three necklaces would grace the breast of her gown. "Don't loom, dear. Sit down. Tell me all about this fall."

Liza glanced out the window at the boxwood maze, but Gilbert had not emerged. She perched on the edge of the chair at her desk. "The youngest daughter. Cassandra."

"Yes, I remember her name. How terrible for her. Was she much injured?"

"Broken limbs The doctor is concerned about the injury to her head. She was unconscious for several minutes."

"Poor child. She will be in great pain. Has the doctor given her laudanum? That is what Doctor Grigsby gave me for pain."

"Laudanum, yes. What brings you here, Mother? I sent my weekly letter yesterday morning, a frank I could have saved if I'd known you were coming."

"Your grandfather will have to forward it to me, then. I missed you. You have not returned to the Towers since you left in May. I decided, on a whim, to visit, and here I am."

"A journey from Sheffield to Wellesbourne Montford is hardly a whim. You also said that Gilbert Meaney proposed this journey."

"He did put me in mind of how much time had passed since last we spoke. Letters say so much but never enough. Before your marriage, we were never apart, except for your years at that school in Bath to which your grandfather insisted on sending you."

Liza leaned an arm over the back of the chair and rested her chin on her wrist. The maze had still not given up Gilbert. He was either lost or waiting a sufficient time for her mother to plow the field that he hoped to plant with his choice of seeds. "And the last three summers, which you spent in Brighton," she pointed out, having learned not to let her mother conveniently forget a truth.

"Yes. I quite enjoyed those visits. You and I should venture somewhere together. Brighton will still be warm, I think, and I did not manage it this year. Or we could go to London. The city is always filled with delights, and the Little Season has commenced. Pack your trunks, and come with me."

Her mother's proposition sounded unusual. "Have you and Grandfather had another falling out?" Her mother's slight grimace came and went, but Liza caught the minuscule change. "You have, haven't you? What was it this time?"

Deborah Corbett gave a moue of distaste, another slight change, for she was not given to mobile expressions that might affect her skin. "He doesn't wish me to have charge of his household."

"Well, Mother, you do have a tendency to dismiss the servants simply because you decide a change is necessary."

"Liza! That is not correct. Besides, Mrs. Dennison wished to leave."

"You fired the housekeeper?"

"No, of course not. I merely suggested a better method—."

"Mrs. Dennison manages the house quite well. What did she do to offend you?"

"You know I have my special diet and the particular ways I like things done."

Liza sighed. "Is Mrs. Dennison still at the Towers?"

"Of course."

That answer meant that Grandfather had reinstated the housekeeper over her mother's objections. Adam Corbett also had his own particular ways, and they had never harmonized with his daughter-in-law. He tolerated temporary problems as long as the wheels soon resumed their well-greased progression on the track he preferred. Liza had finagled situations to give both of them what they wanted most of the time. She dealt with complaints by having excellent reasons as well as little sweeteners ready to placate them.

Liza didn't need more questioning to know what had happened. Grandfather had gone to deal with an issue at one of the far-flung mills. Once he was gone, her mother had fired Mrs. Dennison, who likely viewed the firing as an opportunity for a holiday. Once Grandfather returned, Mrs. Dennison also returned and asked to be re-instated. He would have done that immediately. Then he would have sent for his daughter-in-law and rung one of his thundering tirades over her.

Thwarted in ridding herself of a woman who refused to cater to her foibles, Deborah Corbett had thrown her own tantrum by packing her bags and removing to a hotel.

Only to find that Grandfather would not pay her expenses.

How many bills had she run up in Sheffield?

When had Gilbert Meaney found her and proposed this visit to Myers Montford?

"I did want to visit you." Her mother's plaint sounded like a child denied a treat.

"I am happy to have you visit. While you are here, perhaps we can decide upon a residence for you. Grandfather has suggested several times that you would be happier in a house of your own."

"I will not live in Sheffield. Or York."

"Bath?"

"Certainly not. I wish to become established in London."

"What did Grandfather say to this proposal?"

"He never listens to me."

No, for her plans were never specific enough for him to act upon them. He'd tried to let his daughter-in-law make her own way. That disastrous result had him scooping up the twelve-year-old Liza to come live with him. When Deborah Corbett realized more funds were available if she remained with her daughter and endured her father-in-law, she joined them at the Towers. After a month of her mother's mismanagement followed by constant arguments between mother and grandfather, Liza took over the household, then the gardens, their wardrobes, and her grandfather's cellars and humidors for his cigars.

"It's not five months since I left. How can you two have fallen out so completely?"

She lifted her thin shoulders and dropped them with a sigh. "Your grandfather becomes more stubborn every year."

"If you will leave Mrs. Dennison to manage the household in the way that Grandfather likes, you and he will not have so much dissension."

"I should be able to have the meals that I want without taking them in my room."

The truth finally emerged. They could rehash every misstep or move on. Liza opted to move on, for her mother never changed her mind until days after her mistake was pointed out. "Do you wish my help to plan your new residence, wherever that may be?"

"You planned my Brighton trips so well. Your grandfather didn't quibble about a single expense. I also wanted to see my only daughter," she hastened to add. "Your letters of late have seemed so emotionless."

Reading between the lines of letters that Liza had judiciously crafted didn't sound like her self-involved mother. Had she enlisted Gilbert Meaney? Or had he enlisted her?

How long was this plan in the making? For Greville had said that Gilbert had been in the village for a fortnight. "When did you leave the Towers, Mother?"

"What, dear?" She looked up from digging in her reticule for a lacy handkerchief, dyed to the same Pomono green as her pelisse.

Liza sighed in her turn, not wanting to pursue the questions. Gilbert had manipulated her, but Deborah Corbett would never admit that. What was the outcome he wanted?

Deborah dabbed at her mouth then tucked away the hanky. "I suppose some footman or that butler is listening at the door." She rose and began smoothing on her gloves. "Come walk with me, dear. Show me this puzzle maze."

Liza had no doubt that this walk was part of Gilbert's plan to speak with her alone. Greville had promised to join them. She would leave the garden door open, drawing him outside. He would hear and follow them to the maze.

Her mother's chatter about London occupied their walk from the house and across the lawn.

.~.~.~.

High boxwoods closed around them. Potts' mysterious touch encouraged the plants to a thickly-leaved growth that prevented anyone from seeing from path to path. The grass was kept clipped short. Their gowns drifted over the green blades rather than dragging along the path.

The maze had fascinated Liza from the first day of her arrival, when Clarissa had given her a cursory tour of the house. She had glimpsed it from the nursery window but had no time to find the puzzle's answer. Within a week, though, she'd deciphered the solution, pleasing the head gardener with her quickness. The maze became one of her daily walks. Released from his restraining ribbons, Sparky would bound ahead, and she knew he wouldn't push through the boxwood, growing thick from the ground to three feet over her head. After his run along the paths and into the blind alleys, he came wagging back and took happily to his leash.

At the maze's heart, a bench offered respite, a serene interval which she had needed more often than she liked.

Gilbert waited for them after the second turn of the maze. Liza stopped. Greville could easily find them here. She didn't wish to venture further.

"There you are," Deborah Corbett said. "Now you two can talk in privacy."

"Mother—."

"I will return to the house. Do you suppose that footman will bring tea? I am parched."

She caught her mother's hand. Mr. Vincent's so-called evidence of her half-hour alone with Gilbert was nothing to this. "Do not leave."

"How else can Gilbert speak of his heart to you?"

"I don't—."

She had a return that cut Liza's defense with the truth. "You should not suffer unhappiness, Liza. I know too well what that life is."

Too well she remembered the arguments between her parents. Yes, Deborah Corbett's life with her husband hadn't been happy. Seth Corbett had had his father's big dreams but lacked the necessary business acumen. His wife spent, heedless of the cost because she knew her father-in-law would not allow his son to run up high debts. She hadn't counted on the son not petitioning his father to cover his debts. Shouting and slammed doors had only started their arguments. Liza hid from both parents until calm was restored. Then she crept down, gathered up the bills and I.O.U.'s, tallied them up, and sent a letter to her grandfather.

Her father's death put an end to the arguments but not to the profligate spending. The allowance Adam Corbett provided should have covered their expenses, but at the end of the month the accounts always ran short.

For Deborah Corbett liked to dress well and attend social events, even in mourning, where men would flatter her and coax her to loan them a little money.

"I'm not unhappy," Liza responded now. Even to her the retort lacked conviction.

"You look it."

"My sister-in-law was pushed down the stairs. I'm *worried* for her."

"I worried when Mr. Corbett contracted your marriage to a ne'er-do-well gentleman."

"Greville is not a ne'er-do-well."

"He needed money," her mother said, sounding reasonable and unlike herself. She removed Liza's hand from her own. "He is a fortune hunter."

"His grandfather mortgaged the estate." She omitted much, but she wanted neither her mother nor Gilbert Meaney to have a misreading of Greville.

"I am desperate for a pot of tea," her mother said, as if that ended the problem. For her, it did. She glided away without once looking back.

"I waited here," Gilbert said, as soon as Deborah Corbett took the first turn to leave the maze. "I didn't want Mrs. Corbett to have any difficulty in finding her way out of the maze. She will be fine."

Gilbert motioned for her to come on. Liza had never liked that peremptory gesture from him. It smacked of his belief that he had a right to command her.

"You shouldn't have come." She turned to follow her mother.

He dashed forward and grabbed her arm. His grip hurt, but he relaxed it. "Come with me to the center, so I don't become lost again."

She stared at him, at the heavy fall of his sandy hair, the sprinkling of freckles that she'd once thought made him boyish, at a mouth she'd fantasized as sensual but now looked uncontrolled. His green eyes seemed to smile, but she remembered Victoria's green eyes, lighter than his but filled with poison.

He began to tow her forward, but she balked. "Release me, Gilbert." She repeated it when he dragged her several more steps.

He stopped but kept his grip. "I remember when you desired my company."

She winced at her past foolishness. "You should not have come."

"Your mother wished an escort."

How many times in the past had he lied and she never knew it?

Something rustled in the boxwoods, a bird scratching about for seeds or worms.

"Weren't you already here in Wellesbourne? Masquerading as Bert Manning?"

"How did—? When your mother suggested a visit to you, I naturally came ahead. I thought it best if I assumed a different name while I waited for her."

He recovered quickly. Practiced liars did so.

Liza lifted her gaze to the sky with its illuminating sun, but the heavens gave no immediate answer. "I suppose you're the person who filled her ears with talk of my unhappiness."

"You *are* unhappy. I knew it."

"My transition has been difficult, Gilbert, that I will admit. My husband is *not* the cause of any unhappiness."

"You say that, but do you lie to yourself, Liza? I've seen him in the village. A cold bastard with never a look at lesser mortals like me and like you. He didn't recognize me, you know, though I saw him every day before your wedding. How can you be happy with him?"

"Please release me. You're hurting my arm."

"I have to speak with you."

She searched his eyes but saw nothing. "To what purpose?"

"You married so quickly. I had no chance—."

"You knew what was toward all February and March. You knew when you stayed with us the week before my wedding. You had chances, Gilbert. You did not take advantage of them."

His hand slipped down her forearm to capture hers. He tried to twine together their fingers, but she clenched her hand. He had to settle for wrapping his fingers around her fist. "Forgive me for being a backward man who thought he had no chance with you."

Leaves shook as the bird flew from its cover.

"Why are you here?"

"Your grandfather talks of appointing a general administrator to oversee all of his mills. He plans to step down from constant oversight. His health is failing."

"And you want me to put in a word for you with Grandfather? You think I would give support to a liar."

His face changed. The ugly rictus that seized him frightened her. "Have I lied?"

"I count three lies in the past five minutes. I may have missed one or two more."

He released her. But his hands lifted, as if reaching for her throat.

Liza backed away quickly. "My husband will not be pleased at this threat to me, Gilbert. You should leave. You should not remain in Wellesbourne Montford."

At the word *threat* he shuddered. One hand dropped. The other wiped down his face, wiping away the wrath. She didn't like the narrow-eyed look that remained. He assessed her, measured her against some other yardstick, and decided—what?

"Leave, Gilbert."

"I meant no harm. I—."

"Goodbye."

He hung his head. His shoulders slumped. He looked the image of contrition. Another lie.

She let him precede her. But when he turned the corner of the maze's outer walk, Liza backed a step, then turned toward the interior, needing its solace.

Chapter 18

Birds rustled in the boxwoods.

Hugging herself, Liza wandered along the maze path. The sky had the infinite blue of autumn with no hint of storms, unlike her tumultuous day. After waking in Greville's arms, she had careened from problem to problem, resolving one only to be struck with another.

Gilbert Meaney's unwanted attentions, aided by her mother, ranked as the least of her worries. Mrs. Myers' illogical accusations no longer surprised her. However, Liza hadn't anticipated how strong the woman's hatred was. Even Greville's horrid questions of Victoria did not weigh as heavily as two questions.

Who pushed Cassandra, thinking they pushed me?

Who wants me dead?

Cassandra's fall had absolved her of attempted murder. With that mistake looming, would the murderer give up on killing Liza? Or decide to wait? Let time pass. Let Liza forget to be cautious. Plan the next attempt so it didn't fail.

Liza shivered in the sunbeams and forced her mind away from murderers.

With Mr. Vincent's arrival, would Greville return to thinking she would conspire to murder him?

She paused and looked back, wishing he would appear in the path. He should have joined her by now.

How had Mr. Vincent taken the news of Cassandra's fall?

She stopped and worked out where she was in the maze. The path before her looked blind, but it wrapped around the boxwood hedge before continuing a long run and more turns to gain the center, shifting back and forth like a Greek key. The return behind her had its own series of long runs to the exit. On the right was a blind alley, looking deceptively like the correct route but offering only two paths, each that ended in a wall.

Clarissa would need relief from attending to her sister. Liza needed to return to the house, but she walked deeper into the maze. She didn't want to return to the bland existence of the past months. In two days she had glimpsed a better future. Were all transitions to happiness crowded with questions and apprehension and fears? Was happiness possible without pain?

A dove took flight, trilling a warning. She watched it fly above the green walls and winging across the azure sky.

Go ahead? Turn back?

Leaves rustled, more birds fluttering about. *I might not see as clearly as that infinite blue sky allows, but I refuse to dither.*

She turned back. In doing so, she saved her life.

The attack came from the blind alley. A glinting flash warned her. The flight was downward. She felt a grab at her skirt, a jerk.

And heard a woman curse.

The knife continued its downward slash. It ripped through the fine muslin of her dress. Liza stumbled away. She crashed into the boxwood. The branches embraced her, lifted her upright. In the corner of her eye, dark color shifted. She saw the glinting flash again.

She flew, fleet as the dove.

At the corner, the boxwood hedge cushioned her fall. Then the branches closed around her, clinging arms that tried to trap her for the knife. She still felt that jerk on her dress. She still saw the steely flash. Through sobbing breaths, she heard the murderer's curse. She fought her way free and ran.

Rushing around the corner, she smacked into a solid wall. Hands grabbed her. She scratched and squirmed.

"Dammit, Liza." The hands shoved her away.

She fell to her knees. Sobbing, she scrabbled across the clipped grass.

Hands reached. She slapped them away. She lunged up and fell against the hedge. Raking along the boxwood, she veered around the man and fled.

She ran into another wall, more solid flesh, but the hands didn't hurt as they steadied her. "Good God, Liza." The hands became arms embracing her.

She collapsed against Greville's chest. "Knife," she gasped. "Knife! Behind me!"

He swung her around, putting himself between her and the danger.

She heard a man speak. She heard words but couldn't distinguish them. She burrowed into Greville's chest. She clutched his jacket, his body the sole rock in a shifting world.

"Look what she did to me!"

"Liza. Look at me, Liza."

Those words penetrated her panic. She lifted her head and looked up at Greville, a blurred but strong rock.

"What happened?"

"Knife," she whispered.

"Your arms are scratched."

"The boxwood."

"Good God," he said again, "your dress is torn."

"Knife." She leaned her head against his chest. His heart's steady beat slowed hers.

"Did you do this?"

She kept her face hidden. *Surely he isn't asking me that question?*

"She ran into me. I tried to help her. She clawed me. She drew blood!"

"Did you attack her?"

"Not I."

"Someone did. Look at this." Greville's hand brushed down her side.

"That wasn't me."

His hand heated her lower back as it pressed her against him. "I suppose you are Gilbert Meaney." She counted six heartbeats before the affirmation came. "What are you doing in my maze?"

"Liza and I spoke—."

"She met you there?"

"No," she protested.

"Her mother brought her out to me."

"A little late for you to press your suit, isn't it?" She burrowed closer, and Greville's tightened embrace rewarded her. Gilbert hadn't answered, so Greville bored in with another question. "You're staying in the village as Bert Manning?"

"You've got good sources."

"Yes, I do. A wise man would heed how closely I watch what matters to me."

"Not so closely," Gilbert retorted, "or someone wouldn't have attacked her with a knife."

Greville didn't breathe for a couple of heartbeats, then he conceded, "Your point. Liza, look up. Did you see who attacked you?" He created a little space between them, but one arm still clamped her close.

"N-n-o." Her teeth chattered. "I didn't see her. I heard her."

"Her? You're certain?"

"She cursed when she missed me."

"And these scratches?" His fingers grazed along one arm. "Did he attack you?"

"I fell into the boxwood. He didn't attack me. It was a woman."

Which woman? Victoria? My mother-in-law? Someone unknown? Someone she hadn't expected. Wearing dark clothes. She hadn't recognized the voice. Could anyone have recognized that snarl?

Greville pressed her away. She clung. "I want to search the maze, Liza. Your attacker could still be in there."

"Don't leave me. Please don't. Please, Greville." She sounded weak, and she didn't care. "She will come after you."

"I hope she will." Yet he remained with her, guiding her out of the maze, Gilbert trailing behind them.

A gardener who had heard the commotion ran for Potts when they emerged from the maze. Gilbert agreed to watch and seize whoever tried to flee. Greville ushered her to his study.

As they crossed the terrace, his arm supporting her back, Liza stared at the shattered paving stones, not yet replaced. The falling urn had seemed like a dream. This moment was real: the woman's curse, that horrid jerk on her dress, the knife slashing down to kill.

.~.~.~.

Huddled under a rug on the faded sofa, Liza sipped the whiskey-laced coffee that Greville had secured for her. Mr. Vincent still goggled his surprise. Winston had disappeared to account for everyone in the house.

Pott's report wasn't welcome. The culprit had waited in the maze. He found where footsteps had paced back and forth, flattening the grass in one of the blind alleys. Escape meant pushing through the boxwoods. Branches were broken, "but they'll mend with next year's growth," he assured them. "We searched the whole maze. No sign of them, sir."

"Thank you, Potts," and Liza echoed her husband's gratitude.

Dr. Chambers took her pulse, offered a balm for her scratches, and peered into her eyes as if he could divine the state of her mind. Then he pronounced her shaky but fit.

"You are certain?" Her husband loomed throughout the examination as if he didn't trust the doctor.

"Mrs. Myers took no serious injury. She may have a nightmare or two, but time will heal that scare. You are very lucky, ma'am."

Luck. She remembered how she had turned back in the very second that the woman struck. "God's hand, Dr. Chambers, not random chance."

"True, true." He repacked the contents of his medical bag.

Greville loomed like a protective wall, shoulders square and feet braced wide. "How is my sister?"

"I still have concerns about the head injury. The nurse understands the case. She'll send for me if things worsen. I don't expect them to do so. The young are resilient, and Miss Cassandra before this day has delighted in excellent health."

"Her broken bones?"

"I also expect them to heal without difficulty. Time will tell, though. I can foresee her having no repercussions from these injuries, if she follows my dictates. Miss Myers assures me that her sister is most concerned about dancing at parties when she debuts. That will not be a difficulty, once she heals."

"And she will heal?"

"As I said, the head injury needs close watching. We should know in a couple of days if there will be any lingering effects." He latched the medical bag. "Your mother informs me that she will be removing to the Dower House."

Liza looked up at her husband.

He returned her solemn gaze. "She has expressed that desire."

"Be good for her. She'll have to make decisions rather than depend so heavily on others. She'll also have more scope for interactions. That will prevent her brooding. Now, I must take my leave. I shan't return until the morning. You," he pointed a finger at Liza, "get rested. Best cure for you." He picked up the cumbersome black bag and strode out.

.~.~.~.

Greville traced the edge of a scratch on Liza's arm. "This came too close today," he whispered. "I do not want you hurt. Perhaps we should visit London or the seashore, the two of us alone, until this dies down."

She lifted her head from its pillow on his shoulder. "Only for the attacks to resume on our return? Leaving will not solve the problem, Greville. Whoever this person is, they will wait—or follow us."

His fingers encircled her wrist. "There is that. Our only guarantee is to catch this person. Without evidence we must catch them in the act, and I won't risk you. If we sent them away—."

"Who do you think it is?"

He remained silent.

"Could this person be associated with Gilbert Meaney?"

"Meaney did try to disguise himself as Bert Manning. Yet what reason would he have for killing you? For what purpose? A mad revenge because you refused to marry him?"

"He never asked me to marry him."

"No, I got in first. Why did he come today?"

She lifted up, bracing on her elbows on the mattress. "I don't know. It doesn't make sense. He said that my grandfather plans to appoint a general administrator over the mills, and he wants my recommendation. But, Greville, Grandfather wouldn't listen to anything *I* said about the business. I know very little about running a mill."

"You're his blood. That counts a great deal."

"If I had married Gilbert, yes. By that reckoning, though, you could take charge of his mills."

"Thank you, but no. The estate is trouble enough. Your Mr. Meaney takes a strange way to recommend himself to Mr. Corbett. He's been staying in the village for a fortnight or longer. That's a long time to be away from his job managing a mill."

"See? It's all very strange." She lowered her head, placing her ear over his strong heartbeat. "Do you think the attacker is Victoria?"

"I have no proof."

"But."

"Yes, wife, we have this *but*. I intend to speak with her father on the morrow. If Victoria is sent away before real harm occurs—."

"Cassandra wasn't real harm?"

His fingers tightened on her wrist. "You see my problem." His chest rose and fell, but she heard no change in his heartbeat. "She might never have contemplated murder without my brother Stanton's death."

"I don't understand. I know he was murdered. You did say that once. Yet you did not discover that until last year ... ." Her voice trailed away, wanting answers but not wanting to ask.

"No one knew Stanton was dead. For a decade we all thought he had just abandoned his obligations to his family, to the young woman he left pregnant. My father refused to let me have charge of the estate. He didn't want Stanton to think I'd usurped his place. We fell into greater debt from my father's continued mismanagement. He died thinking his heir cared nothing for his family or inheritance. Then last year, they discovered Stanton's body, on property belonging to that young woman."

"How did they know he was murdered?"

"He had a bullet hole in his skull."

She didn't know what to say. She thought of those long years, with the conflicts Greville must have had with his father as he fought the financial drain on the estate. She thought of that young woman and the child—. "What happened to the baby?"

"It didn't survive."

"Ten long years." He said nothing. She splayed her fingers over his ribcage. "While you grieved for him, you must have also felt great relief that you could at last more forward."

The arm around her shoulder tightened. "Exactly that. My mother plunged into mourning. Stanton was her favorite." The words dropped like stones and sank just as deeply. He had never talked about how hard his own transition was, just the effect on his family. The steps to be taken, the straits to avoid—by marrying her.

She listened to his heartbeat and counted his breaths. Nothing felt resolved. "Ten years, waiting for information about your brother. Ten years, not able to move forward, trying not to sink. Then you receive the news of his death. Victoria must have expected your proposal as soon as the first months of mourning ended. She lays your inattention to being submerged in the estate, seeking loans to keep everything afloat. Then you return from an extended trip to London with the announcement that you will marry in April. Had I been Victoria, I would have thrown something against the wall."

"She would never stoop to an obvious display of emotion."

She remembered an earlier comment designed to cut her and used it now. "How bourgeois."

He rubbed the back of her hand then her fingers, then threaded his longer fingers with hers. "Exactly. The perfect vicar's daughter cannot suddenly vent her rage by screaming about betrayal. Especially since I was very careful to give no grounds for anyone to believe a partiality for her. Victoria might hate me, but she is proud. You would never want anyone to think she depended upon a proposal from her. She is also the serene vicar's daughter, always helpful, always perfect. She can't confess to any struggles with anger, not even to her father. He would counsel Christian love for her rival."

"I see all this. I don't see how it relates to your brother's death."

"His murderer was never caught, Liza. The constable claimed that he could not locate enough evidence. The trail was ten years' cold. Victoria might think a similar ploy would work for her. She has a high opinion of her intellect. If she leaves no evidence—and she hasn't, not any that we can find. She would never confess. The only solution— since our leaving would delay another attempt—is to send her far enough away that she cannot easily return and hope she doesn't fix upon someone else."

"Fix upon? That sounds like an obsession."

"It has to be. It's not reasonable."

The words conjured his mother. Liza swallowed and tackled the harder problem. "Is that the reason you suggested your mother remove to the Dower House?"

"Partly. She could choose to remain here. She would have to treat you as my wife deserves to be treated, as you deserve to be treated for your own self. You offer her courtesy; she offers rudeness. Since she refuses to see that, since she refuses to think, then she will be happier away from my home. We will all be happier."

Foreseeing a problem, Liza lifted up again. "Cassandra can't leave, not until Dr. Chambers says she may."

He tweaked her loose hair. "That will be several months. By then, she may decide she will remain with us rather than live with our mother."

"And Clarissa?"

"Clarissa has requested to remain with us. She has her debut to think of."

"Greville! Clarissa is not so materialistic!"

"Her words, not mine. The debut will also influence Cassandra." He tugged her hair, pulling her closer.

Liza held back. "Your mother will need to join us in London. She cannot be absent from her daughters' debuts."

"By Spring, Mother may tire of this harpy role she designed for herself. She may beg us to allow her to join us in London—but I won't raffle off tickets on the chance. Now, I have better pursuits than talking about Victoria and my mother and sisters."

Liza, blushing, offered him a kiss.

Chapter 19

Monday, 6 September 1813

"Victoria informed us that Miss Cassandra had fallen." The vicar motioned to the upholstered chair before his desk then sat in his own, a straight-backed wooden chair that fit his ascetic personality. "How fares your sister this morning?"

Greville glanced at the paneled door to ensure it remained shut. He didn't want this interview with Pethbridge interrupted by his wife or his daughter. Disdaining the comfortable chair, he stationed himself at the windows.

The heavy curtains were drawn to reveal the garden that swept down to the brook. Willow branches swayed in the gusting wind. Ducks paddled in the water. A cat licked her paws beside a potted flower, its purple blooms cascading. His first words would ruin this idyll.

Throughout his ride, he'd practiced several speeches. To introduce his suspicions, he needed a gentle breeze, not a gusty wind. As he cantered toward the vicarage on the edge of the village, far back from the Romanesque church, he had decided on a blunt announcement. Yet faced with the cleric's gentle features, he delayed, saying only that he had a private matter to discuss. Now he continued to delay.

"I saw Dr. Chambers on my morning constitutional. He was reluctant to discuss your sister's condition. Of course, the doctor is always chary with his prognoses."

Greville turned from the window. "My last intention is to cause you and your wife pain, but I have grave concerns, Rev. Pethbridge, and I can no longer postpone presenting them to you."

"Because you believe Victoria responsible for Cassandra's fall? As well as the attempt on your wife's life? Victoria told us when she returned. This morning she refused to leave her room." His gaze lifted to the ceiling with its ornate plaster decorations. "She intends to leave the district. She believes she has no future in Wellesbourne Montford. I must agree with her. She is quite distressed that you harbor these suspicions"

"Your daughter is not the only person distressed by the events of the past few days."

"Yes, I did explain that to her." His benign expression became pained. "She cannot sow discordant seeds without reaping a whirlwind of wrath. I have surprised you, I see, but I know my daughter very well, Mr. Myers. My wife and I have repeatedly cautioned her, first when she set her aspirations to become Mrs. Myers of Myers Montford, and then when she determined that making herself indispensable to the dowager would create a wedge between your bride and your family."

"She succeeded at the latter. She infected my mother and younger sister with an unreasonable animosity. I can only hope that, with time and maturity, Cassandra will overcome her antagonism. My mother likely will not."

The vicar linked his fingers and rested them before him on the desk. "Your mother has often exhibited a tendency to take unreasonable dislikes to people or events, and nothing will change her opinion. For that reason, her removal from the household is your wisest course."

The reverend had a better understanding of the two principals in his flock than Greville had credited. The man's gentle nature and tendency to look for the good had often exasperated him over the years. Perhaps he shouldn't have so quickly dispensed his opinion. "Starting today, the Dower House will be opened. Before this week is through, it should be ready for occupancy."

"And what of my daughter?"

"What do you suggest?"

"If she remains in daily contact with your mother, the two of them will only feed each other poison. In this respect, Miss Cassandra's injuries offer an opportunity for the distance and growth your sister needs to overcome the venom that infected her. I assume your wife offers a hand in caring for her?"

Liza had proposed this morning to tend Cassandra while the nurse had relief after her night's vigil. "She does."

"God's mysterious ways. This event will open your sister's eyes to your wife's kindness and temperate disposition. Your mother will eventually see her error. She cannot fail to do so. So we dispense with your immediate issues and turn to mine. My wife had a suggestion this morning, over our breakfast. Victoria needs the same time and maturity that we hope will alter Miss Cassandra. My own sister resides in Manchester where she manages a mission for the workers. Victoria could have charge of the school."

Greville sank into the upholstered chair. "Will she not view her relegation to a mission schoolroom as punishment rather than opportunity?"

The vicar rubbed the crease between his whitening brows. "Victoria is not a crusader, I agree. At the moment, if I may be common, she wants the bit between her teeth and a yard of tin to blow her freedom to the world. Perhaps my sister is not the best choice. Victoria does not often volunteer to work with the children of this parish. A waste of her education. My other suggestion is that she take residence with my wife's brother, in Cambridge. That will be a more acceptable situation for her, and it may prevent her from ruining herself entirely. She will find many more opportunities for her future in Cambridge. After our small village, Cambridge's scope may seem more a reward than a separation caused by her seeds of discord. We do not wish to reward her sins. I will leave this decision to you, Mr. Myers, since your family is the one most affected. Which solution will be more acceptable to you?"

"I am only concerned with my wife's safety, Rev. Pethbridge."

"As it should be your primary focus, sir, but you remain under a misapprehension. My daughter did not cause Miss Cassandra's fall nor the accident with the urn."

Greville leaned forward. He rested a fist on the desk's edge. "She was there, both times. She was the only person in the house who could have pushed Cassandra."

"Your sister could simply have fallen."

"She was pushed."

The vicar's gaze didn't waver. "Not my Victoria."

"I suppose this is what she claims."

"It is. I believe her. I know she is my daughter, and a father is inclined to believe his children. I know Victoria can be malicious when she is thwarted. Nevertheless, she does not have a vicious heart. She is not a murderess."

"Not yet."

"I am her spiritual guide, Mr. Myers. I know what my daughter is capable of. Victoria would not commit murder."

"You have no proof of her innocence as I have no proof of her guilt."

"True." He grasped the wooden cross laying on his chest. "My daughter says that she was not the only person in your house yestermorn. Several servants were there as well as a man she did not know."

"A man she didn't know?" Gilbert Meaney flashed into his mind. "Who?"

"She has no idea. She saw his reflection in a mirror."

"Victoria said nothing yesterday."

"The shock of finding Cassandra drove it from her mind. When she did remember, your accusations had angered her."

"I want to talk to her. I want a description of this man."

"My daughter, however, does not wish to speak to you."

"Your daughter has no choice. She will give me his description or—." Greville stopped. He jerked upright and strode to the door. He even touched the knob only to realize he could not force Victoria to tell him anything. She was no weak miss who would bow under his questions. With no reason to stay in his good graces, she was willful enough to wish him to the devil and refuse to say another word. "I *have* to know—."

He stopped again. His father's ultimatums hadn't worked with Stanton. They'd driven his brother to sever ties, refusing to contact them until his last letter, weeks before his death, filled with the young woman he planned to marry.

His own ultimatum with Cassandra hadn't worked.

"I need the man's description." He turned to see the vicar's strange smile.

"She gave it to me." He opened the narrow drawer above the kneehole and extracted a paper which he passed across the desk.

Brown hair. Brown eyes. Not overly tall or short. Brown suit. "This isn't helpful."

"No, I agree. However, she said he was kissing one of your maids. You should question your servants."

He had left the questions to Winston. He should do that himself. He would, as soon as he returned, starting with the servants who hadn't attended church. "If I brought the man here, would Victoria be willing to identify him?"

"Do you have an idea who this stranger is?"

"A man named Gilbert Meaney, who has a room at the pub under the name Bert Manning."

. ~ . ~ . ~ .

Cassandra scowled. "I don't want broth."

"You will find it nourishing." Liza kept her voice mild. Cassandra had rejected this morning's gruel and only drunk the tea. Now she rejected the broth that the nurse had ordered.

"I am hungry."

"Indeed, you must be, for you slept through much of yesterday and had only tea this morning. Nurse Jeffries ordered this for you. She is following the diet that Dr. Chambers recommended."

"I thought you ordered it."

"No. I do not wish to interfere in Dr. Chambers' dictates."

"Mama hasn't come to see me." Cassandra closed her eyes. "Did Greville send her away?"

Liza thought of Greville's plan to move his mother to the Dower House. "No, she's still here." That wasn't a lie. It would be a week or more before Mrs. Myers took residence in the village.

"Why hasn't she come to see me? Greville came this morning. He cried when he saw me."

"Cassandra—."

"He didn't want me to see. He turned away, but I saw him wipe his eyes."

Liza stared at the broth. She could not say that Greville cared for Cassandra because a brother was honor-bound to care for his sister. What would that suggest about their mother? "Your brother only wants what is best for you. I think," she continued hurriedly, "a little scrambled egg and cooked apple would go well with this broth? You should drink the broth, for it will help your bones to knit. Cook tended it all night."

"She did?"

"Yes. Everyone wants you to recover, Cassandra. Everyone is concerned about you. Shall I have Cook send up egg and apple?"

"And one of her sweet pastries?"

"Let's see how the egg and apple and broth do."

The sweet pastry remained uneaten, for the light meal followed by a dose of laudanum soothed the pain of the broken bones and allowed Cassandra to sleep.

Liza reached across to remove the bed tray. The young woman opened bleary eyes. "You're good to me."

"Hush now, you need to sleep."

"I said awful things about you."

"I think we shall move past that. We can, can't we?"

When Cassandra murmured and closed her eyes, Liza thought she drifted to sleep, but before she set the tray outside the room, her younger sister-in-law spoke again, her voice hushed and blurred. "How did you scratch your arms?"

She glanced at the scratches and remembered yesterday's terror. "I fell into a boxwood. Sleep now, Cassandra."

Tillie Sparrow waited in the hall. She took the tray. "Will you be with her the whole day, ma'am?"

"Clarissa will spell me this afternoon."

"You should get sunshine, ma'am. Be good for your soul."

"I will. Not the maze, though." She shivered at the memory of flashing metal.

"That roof's got a good view, and you can walk all the way around."

"Do you like the roof walk, Sparrow?"

"It's private, and not much else is private for a servant. One of them scratches don't look good, ma'am."

Liza covered the angry streak with her hand. "I have an ointment to use."

"Shall I bring you a tray for your luncheon?"

"I will be joining Clarissa for luncheon. Tell Mrs. Timmons that the cinnamon in the apple was much appreciated. Thank you, Sparrow."

She shut the door and returned to her station beside the window, but the garden didn't attract her eyes. She stared at the inflamed scratch. Her heart sped up its pace as she remembered the knife. That snarl, nearly unrecognizable as a woman's voice. *Who hates me that much?*

She wished Greville would return from his mission to the village.

.~.~.~.

"Mr. Manning's not here, sir, as I told you."

"Open the door," Greville ordered.

The pub host inserted his key, jiggled it then turned the lock. He entered the room first. Greville ducked his head as he wedged his shoulders through the narrow door. Constable Cooper crowded his stocky form behind him.

A grip valise rested on the single chair. The quilt and bedlinens were folded back. Patchwork curtains fluttered in the window.

"The girl's been through," the host said, "seeing to things."

Greville opened the valise and shoved his hand through folded clothes. "When did he leave?"

"After breakfast, sir. Walking."

He turned away from the valise, and the constable started his own check. Greville stared around the room. Where could he find evidence of this man's identity? "You are certain, Constable, that this man is the only stranger in the village?"

"Yes, sir. Bert Manning's his name. Been here long enough that most people recognize him even if they don't know his name. He smoked a pipe with me last evening."

"What did he talk about?"

"Prospects, sir." Constable Cooper shut the valise. He bent to the narrow bed and ran his hand under the mattress. "He's got a job with better pay ahead of him. Managing several mills for an old curmudgeon whose health is failing."

That wasn't a coincidence; that was Gilbert Meaney bragging his secret plans to a stranger he never expected to meet again. Yet how did he expect to profit? Married, Liza was beyond his reach. *Or does he plan to kill me and then marry her?* He turned back to the host, who stood with folded arms watching the young constable get on his knees to look under the bed. "Where was this Manning fellow last Friday?"

"He sat down there in front of the cold hearth, smoking up my taproom."

"Doing what?"

"Reading. Newspapers first. Then a book. He went to the store early, but he wasn't gone more than a quarter-hour."

Riding to the estate took three times that, twice over for the return trip.

"And the vicar came in. They talked a bit, then him and the reverend went off to the old cemetery. That took an hour of his afternoon, then back they came, and the vicar bent his ear all through tea about tombstone etchings."

Still not enough time. Frustrated, Greville crammed through the door. Constable Cooper followed close, with the host locking the room back before he came down the narrow stairs to join them in the taproom.

"A pint, sir, afore you head back?"

"Half-pint. Give the pint to the constable here," and the young man looked gratified to get a drink he didn't have to pay for. "Do you know where Mr. Manning headed today?"

"Now that I don't, as I told you. He did walk, sir." He slid the glasses across the bar.

The constable took a drink, wiped foam off his lips, then set the pint down with a happy sigh. He shifted his feet. "Any other strangers come in, Hodge, before or after Mr. Manning? Anyone besides the vicar spend time talking to him?"

"No one. Now, he goes on his walks, usually comes back chipper. I don't know if he's been meeting anybody while he's out. The only person I saw him talking to would be that Mrs. Corbett who came on the mail coach late Saturday."

Greville's drink hit the bar hard. "Mrs. Corbett? Mrs. Deborah Corbett?" Why hadn't he wondered how she had arrived in the village?

"That's the one. They had dinner together on Saturday evening. She went to church alone, then he hired my cart to take them out to the estate after."

And no one at Myers Montford recognized the woman because she'd not visited her daughter before. "Where did he go while she went to the church?"

"Walking along the river, he said."

"That's when Miss Cassandra was attacked, wasn't it, sir?" The constable had taken out his notebook and pencil and jotted his notes. The gleam in his eyes revealed his excitement at this case, a change from escorting drunks home from the pub and herding wastrels from one side of the district to another so they didn't stay.

"Yes, and that is also when Miss Pethbridge saw a strange man in my house before she found my sister at the foot of the stairs."

"That's not good, sir. Where is he now, Hodge?"

"Don't know, sir, as I told you. Off on a walk."

"He walks every day except on the day my wife is nearly killed. He gave himself an alibi. He must have a finger in this, sir."

"A finger, yes, but not his hand, not to push my sister and not to push off that urn. I can't determine how my wife's death will benefit him."

"You know anything about this Mrs. Corbett?"

"My mother-in-law. She's staying at the house now."

"That don't look good, sir, her and him."

"Mrs. Corbett wouldn't hurt her own daughter."

"There's them that has. A couple of counties over—."

"Now, now, Hodge." The constable finished his last note and flipped his notebook shut. "This Mrs. Corbett, she wasn't present for the first attempt at murder, and she had an alibi for the second attempt, which mistook your sister, sir. Could she have been in the maze when your wife was attacked?"

"I saw her in the house myself, minutes before. She directed me to my wife." Deborah Corbett had smiled as she informed him that her daughter was walking the maze with Gilbert Meaney. The doubts awakened by Mr. Vincent had lifted their ugly snouts.

"This Mr. Manning—."

"Whose real name is Gilbert Meaney."

"Yes, sir, we'll call him that when his identity is confirmed. Could he have tried to stab your wife?"

Meaney had lurked just outside the maze, clearly waiting.

For his accomplice to succeed at the third attempt? Who was his accomplice? Why did they want to kill Liza?

Chapter 20

"Do come." Clarissa tugged Liza's arm. "You spent the morning tucked away with Cassandra, and I'll spend the afternoon with her. Before then, I want fresh air and distant views, and there's nowhere better than the roof. You never go up there, do you?"

"Sparky doesn't like the height."

"You can take him on the run through the maze this afternoon."

She shuddered. "Not today. Not even this week."

"Then through the gardens. I demand you come with me. Nowhere else will blow away the cobwebs left by venomous spiders. Do come, Liza. I don't want to go by myself. Not today, after all that's happened."

Even knowing Clarissa designed her appeal to manipulate her, Liza allowed herself to be tugged along.

.~.~.~.

The steady canter rocked the solution from its hidden corners.

Liza's grandfather was in ill health. He planned to appoint an administrator over all his mills. The curmudgeon wouldn't turn to his only family, his granddaughter Liza. She'd confessed that she knew nothing about his business. And she was a woman. The hide-bound old man wouldn't think a woman should run a business.

He would turn to a trusted employee, one favored enough to have been invited to his home and to serve as an escort for his eligible granddaughter. Perhaps Adam Corbett would have promoted a match between them if he hadn't spied a gentleman fortune-hunter.

Remove Liza as Adam Corbett's heir, and he would look for an heir who could manage his business. Who better than the administrator, the clever young man he'd favored?

But who was his accomplice?

.~.~.~.

"Liza, I must tell you something."

She slowed her progress, and Clarissa perforce did as well. "What is it, Mother?"

Deborah Corbett pursed her lips as she contemplated Clarissa's arm looped through her daughter's. "It is a matter of some delicacy. This is actually the reason that I came. I would ask that we are permitted privacy."

"I'll go on to the roof," Clarissa offered. "I do not want to miss a minute of this sunshine. Join me when your conversation with your mother is concluded." She slid her arm free, but Liza caught her hand.

"Can it wait, Mother? Clarissa will need to stay with her sister in a half-hour."

"It concerns your father. I was not aware that the matter had resurfaced until a couple of months ago."

"So, this matter has waited for two months. It can wait a half-hour longer. Come, Clarissa," and they started up the stairs to the next floor and above it the box room and its access to the roof.

"I fear you will not be happy with this information about your father," her mother persisted. "I am certain you will be as disappointed in him as I am."

"If I am to be disappointed," she called back, already halfway up the stairs, "all the more reason to delay receiving this news."

"Elizabeth! I think you must hear this. Elizabeth."

"Oh dear, your mother is using your full name. This is serious."

"Not serious enough. As she said, it waited for two months."

"You could ask her to tell you quickly. Only with my mother, nothing ever comes out quickly. Wait, I think she is calling to you."

They paused at the top of the flight. Liza thought her mother said *your sister*. "Do you hear her?"

Clarissa cocked her head. "Not now. Perhaps you should go to her."

"Perhaps she should have told me yesterday."

"Yesterday was Cassandra's fall and the attack on you."

"She could have found time. This morning, when Cassandra was drowsing."

Clarissa opened the box room door. "A matter of some delicacy and about your father. What could it be?"

Liza averted her gaze from the open crate that held the broken bits of her china. Straw littered the floor, trailing from the crate to the open door to the roof. "I must tell Mrs. Grunby to have this removed."

As they picked their way through the trunks and old furniture and past tall portraits and stacked boxes, Clarissa ventured, "A scandalous affair?"

"My father was known for them." Liza heard her sturdy words and wondered when Seth Corbett's multitude of affairs had ceased to concern her. Had time wrought its miracle cure? Or had life jaded her? "After his death, a woman came to our house. She claimed Papa had sent her support for their little girl. Mama swore he'd never done so, that he would never support an illegitimate child, especially a girl."

Clarissa opened the door to the roof. Sunlight poured in. Dust motes floated in the air. Liza stumbled over a broken doll as she followed the path Clarissa had taken.

Cool wind blew in, freshening the close air. Her sister-in-law stepped through the opening. She lifted her face to the blue sky. "Liza, it's glorious today." She offered a hand. "Careful stepping out. I stubbed my toe once and went sprawling."

Liza climbed over the high threshold. The opening looked more fitted for a large window than a door. When she straightened, slate tiles and the azure sky filled her eyes. After the dim interiors, the sun blazed, and she blinked several times. Warm air rose from the roof, shimmering above the tiles.

The box room door opened between the double-hipped roof. Arms out like a circus acrobat, Clarissa traversed the narrow walk between the two sloping roofs. Painted white with splashes on the slate tiles, the wood walk looked blinding.

She gazed around her, trying to identify the chimneys. The great central hearth of the drawing room would be the largest chimney. In the upper stories, several rooms shared the same chimney, for builders considered efficiency over aesthetics. The lady's suite on the first floor would share a chimney with the lord's suite. Where were their rooms?

She hadn't considered the house's plan from the roof down.

"What are you waiting for?" Clarissa had reached the end of the walk and rested a hand on the low parapet that encompassed the roof.

"Do I shut the door?"

"Leave it open. I always do. I close the box room door."

Liza started along the glaring walk. "Do you come up often?"

"In past years I've come every day that the sun shined. Not in winter. Ice covers the walk and collects in patches along the parapet." She steadied Liza's transition from the walk to the parapet. "There. Look at the view! You can see the church's bell tower."

"Where? Oh, there. The village looks so much closer from here." The grey stones of the crenellated Romanesque tower peered over the great oaks and elms of the parkland. A crimson flag flapped above the church tower, as brightly visible as the red breast of a bullfinch in a winter garden. "I didn't know the church flew a flag."

"What?" Clarissa turned quickly, wobbled and grabbed Liza's arm to steady herself. "Usually it's a green flag. I wonder why the vicar changed it."

"Red stands for danger."

"Yes. Something must have happened in the village. I wonder if it's a signal for Dr. Chambers. Look. See that dark line winding through the parkland. It's a break in the trees. That's our drive."

Liza did see the break, like a dark green ribbon winding through the treetops with their first show of autumn color.

"The road beyond the parkland loops as well, to follow the river to the mill and the bridge, before cutting back to the village. Come around this way. You'll have a wonderful view of the estate. See that gutter, how the stone is darker there. The water runs off the roof there. In the winter, that will be pure ice, so never come up in winter, Liza. It's dangerous. Or when the wind is up. I love it when the clouds are rushing in and the wind is tearing them apart. I wish I could capture that on canvas, but it's beyond my skill."

"I like the flowers you paint."

"Thank you. Here. Don't look down." She swept her arm wide. "Look at this instead."

The vista revealed the reasons Clarissa retreated to the roof. The tiled roofs of the closer buildings were like red patches in an ocean of green. The long stable with its cupolas broke the vista. A wall between the manor grounds and the patchwork fields beyond. More terra cotta roofs on farm buildings rather than the thatch. A wagon climbed a distant hill. Around it, workers buzzed, droning bees who gathered the cut hay. In another field the workers scythed a cereal crop, and pickers harvested in the orchard beyond. Pastures ran parallel, taking the higher grounds more difficult for the plow. Cows and sheep grazed the steeper slopes.

"I remember Greville drove you over the estate when you first arrived, but this really gives you the range of our land."

"Where is the weir, the one that he rebuilt?"

"On the other side. Do you want to see it?"

"I want to see everything!"

"We just follow the parapet around then. After you."

Liza shook her head, still unsteady. "I'm slow," she explained. The wind snatched her words and tossed them beyond the parapet.

Clarissa laughed and went ahead.

.~.~.~.

Greville galloped out of the parkland, the constable behind him on a borrowed hack. The grey stones of the house looked gloomy against the cloudless sky. Two women carefully walked along the parapet. Clarissa he expected, for she often escaped to the roof. The following woman wore mint green, the color Liza had chosen this morning.

They reached the corner. Clarissa paused and half-turned.

A figure lunged from the cover of the gable and swung a long stick.

Clarissa fell back. Liza grabbed her. For a horrible second, they teetered, then his sister collapsed, falling behind the parapet, out of his sight.

"Don't shout, sir," the constable warned. Greville didn't realize that he had, but his throat felt ripped open. "Don't distract her."

Liza was inching backwards as the other—a woman—stepped over his sister. The woman paused, jerking at her skirt as if something had caught it.

"How do we get up there, sir?"

He didn't answer, just spurred his hunter.

A footman opened the door as he flung off the sorrel horse. He rushed past the servant and plunged into the dim interior.

"Sir? Sir, what has happened?"

He thrust Winston aside. "Fetch Potts. Fetch Marshall." He raced for the stairs. "Liza's on the roof! Someone's attacking her. Constable!"

"Behind you, sir. Keep going!"

.~.~.~.

Tillie Sparrow jerked her skirt free of Clarissa's grip. She kicked at the young woman then swayed and grabbed the gable to steady herself. Liza backed away.

The maid held a cricket bat, splotched red with Clarissa's blood. She stepped past and smiled, and Liza shivered.

"You can't escape. No use trying, little Miss Perfect."

Liza considered running down the walk between the roofs. It offered safety from falling. Yet she didn't dare turn her back on the maid. She passed the white-washed boards and continued on, reaching for the next sloping gable. If she could stay back far enough, Greville would come. She'd heard his shout, seen him jump from his big hunter as it skidded, the gravel sliding beneath the iron hooves.

"Why do you want to kill me? It's been you, hasn't it? Who are you?" Then her mother's delicate matter shifted into a new focus. "Are you one of my father's by-blows?"

"You're quick, dear sister. His *only* by-blow. He used to come to see me before he died. I had sweets to eat, and my own maid, and pretty dresses to wear. My mama wore pretty dresses, too. That all stopped when he died, thanks to your mother."

"But you want to kill *me*."

"Of course." She sounded so matter of fact that Liza knew Tillie didn't need hate to motivate her. Her actions were colder than hate, filled with merciless intent.

"I suppose you introduced yourself to Grandfather."

"Gilbert did."

The roof edge came back to her hand as the gable sloped downward. She would soon reach the corner. *How long before Greville reaches the roof?*

"Gilbert's waiting in the box room, ready to stop your loving husband."

"No!"

"Yes." And Tillie laughed, a bell-like trill of happiness.

"Do you think Grandfather will bequeath all his wealth to you? Tillie, they will hang you."

"They have to figure out it was me. No one here knows my name or where I'm from. Only you know I'm your half-sister."

"Gilbert knows."

Without the roof's protection, the wind struck hard. Liza teetered at the corner. Along this side, the roof sloped away from the low parapet She passed a pediment that had supported the cast-stone urns. It offered a steady brace until Liza backed another step. Her hand slipped from the square pediment. She turned the corner and felt backwards for her next step.

Tillie took a long step, gaining inches that Liza needed to stay out of the cricket bat's swing.

"Has Gilbert helped you at all?"

"Not he. He says if I want it badly enough, I've got to do it. So I am. Never again will I grub for someone else. Never again will I do anything to fill my belly. I'll be eating sweets and wearing silks in a month, you see if I don't."

"You don't have to kill me," she reasoned. "Grandfather could divide his property. It would still be more than enough."

"Too late to do that now. Besides, I don't share. I *never* share. If you'd married Gilbert like you were supposed to, then we wouldn't have had all this trouble. A fall at a coaching inn, and everyone's so sad, your grandfather most of all. Who's he going to leave all his money to? There I am, all demure and innocent. His son's blood in my veins for all that I'm his by-blow. I'll have it all while you rot in your grave."

Two quick strides covered the distance between them. She swung the bat.

Liza ducked. She fell onto the angled roof. The slate clattered as she hit. Pieces skittered away from her scrabbling hands.

Tillie took another long step forward. Looming over Liza, she raised the bat.

.~.~.~.

The man plowed into Greville, knocking him into a crate. He hit the wood hard, losing his breath. A fist punched low on his back.

He shoved off the crate as the man drove in. Force met impetus, and the man staggered. Greville wheeled and punched. His fist connected. Blood spattered. The man fell backward.

"Go, go, sir!" Constable Cooper twisted the man's arm behind his back. "Get to your wife."

Greville lunged through the open door.

Sunlight blinded him, but he surged ahead, his steps sure as he ran to the parapet.

He turned left.

Clarissa had levered up. Blood covered her head, but she pointed the other way.

He whirled around and ran for the other corner. As the gable roof dropped, he saw a cricket bat lifting. The gusty wind whipped the woman's hair and the soot-colored skirts of her maid's uniform.

Liza lay on the slate tiles. Even as he lunged for the bat, his wife whipped around an arm. She slashed across the maid's midriff as he grabbed the paddle-like bat and wrenched it free.

The woman screamed. Her wind-streamed hair blew over her face, hiding it. Blood seeped from her stomach.

She pressed her hands to her belly. "How? How? Why?" Lifting her hands, she stared at the blood. "You bitch." Then she laughed, a weird trill that cascaded down. When it died, she looked blank, stiff and white as a mask. "Me rotting in the grave." And she stepped off the parapet.

She dropped without a sound.

Greville didn't look. He knelt beside Liza. "Are you hurt? Please tell me you're not hurt. What did you use on her?"

She opened her hand. A sharp wedge of slate dropped to the roof.

Chapter 21

The slate had sliced her palm. As he wrapped his handkerchief around her hand, Liza shuddered. "Is she—?"

"Doubtless." He finished the knot then levered up. Grasping her elbows, he lifted her upright then embraced her as tightly as he'd tied the handkerchief.

She sank against him. His grip controlled her shuddering body. She said something, muffled against his chest. Greville eased his grip so Liza could lift her head.

"Clarissa?"

"Injured but alive."

"She saved my life. She grabbed Tillie, held her long enough that I could get a few feet away from her."

He had dozens of questions, but they would wait.

"Sir! Ma'am! Thank God!" Winston clung to the line of the roof. The wind whipped up his wispy hair and tore at his neat coat. "Ma'am, are you injured?"

"She will be fine," Greville answered for her. "My sister?"

"James is leading her along the walk, sir. She looks bad, sir."

Greville steadied Liza as he started their return to the safer corner of the roof. "Dr. Chambers will tell us the damage. He'll need to be sent for."

Winston backed up, keeping a hand on the gable. "He arrived a bare minute behind you, sir. Hodge, the pub host, he sent him."

"The man in the box room, Winston?"

He felt Liza's start. She whispered, "Gilbert Meaney" even as the butler said, "Constable Cooper has him in custody. It's the man who came with Mrs. Corbett yesterday, sir."

"Constable Cooper will wish to view the maid's body. See her covered then taken to the church. She's in the hands of the vicar and the sexton now. Tell the constable that he can return tomorrow for any statements he needs. We've had enough today."

"Yes, sir."

"See that Potts and Marshall and a couple of other strong men accompany the constable and his prisoner to gaol."

"Indeed, sir. I believe they are eager to see the man behind a steel door." He trotted along the narrow walk and crammed through the roof door, quickly disappearing.

Liza didn't release her clutching grip on Greville's hand and arm until she stood in the box room. He yanked the door shut. The room darkened, the only illumination from the open stairway door.

"Is it over?"

"Yes."

She wept then.

.~.~.~.

Dr. Chambers dabbed at the seeping blood across Liza's palm. "I have stitched her scalp," he said of Clarissa. "She'll have a headache for a while, but no real damage, barring any infection. The scar won't show, as it's under her hair."

"Thank you, God. She saved my life, Doctor."

His eyes crinkled. "And quite proud of herself for it."

"Will there be lasting damage to Liza's hands?" Greville asked. "She plays the piano beautifully, Doctor. I make a point to listen whenever she plays." He picked up her right hand, clenching on the arm of his sofa while the doctor probed the flesh that the slate had sliced open. "From now on, I will leave my door open, and you will join me afterwards for an early tea. Yes?"

She gave a decided nod then jerked as Chambers' inspection hurt.

"I must ask that you hold her hand tightly, Mr. Myers."

Liza started to look at her injured hand then resolutely turned her head away. "Will I need stitches?"

"A few." He plucked something from the cut and dropped it on the small table brought over to the sofa to hold his implements. "Mrs. Myers, you are not going to enjoy the next few minutes," and he removed the stopper on a brown bottle. "My own remedy."

Liza flinched and cried during the application of the fiery tincture. Greville also held her arm while Dr. Chambers plied his needle in several stitches to close the open flesh. Then he nestled his wife close as she sobbed. Chambers calmly rolled up the unused lengths of cloth and gauze.

When he shut his medical bag, he leaned back. "I certainly didn't expect to be setting bones and stitching wounds after I left the Army. Nor do I want to return to tend another Myers lady."

"You won't," Greville swore.

"I'll examine Miss Cassandra before I leave. Keep that bandage dry and clean, Mrs. Myers. Early tomorrow I will return to check on all my patients. I advise rest for the remainder of this day. A couple of glasses of whiskey might help your wife, sir."

Sniffing into Greville's handkerchief, Liza ignored the doctor. "She'll rest," he swore.

. ~ . ~ . ~ .

Liza's retreat to rest was delayed, for when Greville led her from his study to the stairs, Mr. Vincent lurked there.

"Sir! Mrs. Myers, I must express—Good God!" he exclaimed at her blood-covered gown and her tear-ruined face.

"You need to wait, Vincent." He didn't stop. He kept Liza moving with his arm at her lower back. "My wife needs quiet and rest after her ordeal."

"Sir, it's a matter—. I have spoken with Mrs. Corbett. When I saw the man arrested by the constable and—well, sir, I must offer my deepest apologies to your wife." Liza's steps slowed. When she looked her unspoken questions at the wizened man, a spate of words broke free. "Mrs. Myers, I fear I have taken false reports of your character and intentions. I had inquired, prior to your marriage and afterwards, and I believed lies, scurrilous lies about your reasons for agreeing to this marriage. I should have interviewed Mr. Corbett himself as well as yourself, ma'am. And your mother. I can only express my sincerest apologies."

She stopped at the bottom of the steps. Looking at the long flight, she sighed. "I could have rested on that sofa in your office, Greville. It's quite comfortable."

"It's not, as I have reason to know. Trust me, were you resting on it an hour from now, you would wish you were in your own bed."

She heaved a great sigh. Obviously wanting to delay the climb, she looked again at Vincent. "Scurrilous lies?"

The man's face flamed. "Mr. Myers has enlightened me as to the falsity of the chief lie—."

"I do not think we need to repeat any of that," Greville growled, and Liza tightened her grip.

"No, I think not," she agreed, and Vincent's relief washed him chalky white. "Tell me, Mr. Vincent, how did you come to understand your mistake?"

"The man Gilbert Meaney. Since he obviously had worked in concert with the woman who attacked you and Miss Myers, the constable demanded that he identify her. Once I heard her name, all came clear. And then, at my questions, Meaney admitted that he lied to my investigator, not only in his statements but in giving his name as Guilford Manley."

"Your investigator did not think to check the veracity of the man's report or identity?"

He winced at that gibe. "Mr. Myers, I promise to have words with the man on the importance of such checks. His report seemed legitimate, as it was verified by a Miss Matilda Robbins. Next time I will demand twice that number of checks."

Liza sagged against him. "I fear I am losing the thread of this. Who is Matilda Robbins?"

"You know her, ma'am, as Tillie Sparrow. Your mother has the rest of the pertinent information, Mrs. Myers. She confirms the woman as your father's illegitimate daughter."

"Greville, I can take no more of this."

"As you wish, my heart."

She gasped when he lifted her and started up the stairs. "You will fall. I'm too heavy."

"Nonsense," a reply that answered both complaints.

Her maid had the curtains drawn and the bed linens pulled down, but she directed him to a chair in the dressing room. "For my lady needs out of that gown. You'll stay to steady her, sir?"

"I shan't faint, Mercy."

"No, ma'am, that you won't, but getting this gown off may hurt."

"Cut it off," Greville advised, and Mercy fetched scissors.

As the maid snipped at a shoulder, Liza leaned her head against his torso. "I suppose we can't save this gown?"

"Not with all that blood, ma'am, no."

"I do like this gown."

Greville cupped her head, threading his fingers into her fallen curls. "You may buy another. You may buy a round dozen." She giggled softly, and he knew the whiskey had kicked in.

The maid applied herself to the other shoulder and soon the gown was puddled on the floor. When Liza was down to her shift, Greville again lifted her. He placed her carefully in the bed and drew the covers up. "Do you want a window open?"

"A little," and Mercy hastened to obey.

His fingers grazed her cheek. "Sleep. All will be well now."

Her uninjured hand caught his. "I liked being called *your heart*. Will you come tonight?"

"We shouldn't—."

"I like knowing you're here."

The whiskey had relaxed her tongue, freeing a truth that she would have hidden. He vowed to get a couple more whiskeys in her sometime soon. "I will be here."

"Good." Her dark lashes swept down. Exhausted by the adrenaline that had spurred her defense, worn out by Dr. Chambers' treatment, and relaxed by the whiskey, Liza fell quickly into sleep.

He stood over her, watching her sleep, until the maid finished cleaning up and returned with a tray and a kettle, which she set by the fire, ready to make tea when her mistress awoke.

"I'll keep watch, sir."

"Send for me, as soon as she asks."

"I will. Now, off with you. Check on those sisters of yours, sir."

1814

Epilogue

Monday, 3 April ~ Grosvenor Square, London

Clarissa peered into a looking glass. "Are you certain no one will see the scar?"

Liza fastened the clasp on Cassandra's double-strand choker of pearls. "It's had six months to heal. It's so faint that no one will see it even if they look closely. Besides, your curls hide the scar."

"You have nothing to fear, Rissa." Cassandra pouted. "As soon as I start dancing, everyone will see I'm a cripple."

"Hardly that." Greville leaned a shoulder on the jamb. He snared his wife's gaze. They shared a smile. She wore a grey gown of shimmering silver that reminded him of an illuminated moon. Her baby bump did not yet show beneath the empire waist. "Those caper merchants we hired swore that no one would notice your limp."

"They only said that because you employed them."

"Then keep your head up," he advised, "and when people gossip, tell them that someone tried to murder you."

"That's heartless," the elder Mrs. Myers remonstrated.

"Indeed, that may be the answer," Liza quietly agreed with her husband. "People will talk. You must direct their talk. Make yourself the heroine."

"I'm the heroine," Clarissa objected. "I saved Liza's life. You can tell them how the murderous Tillie focused on you and then all about your days and days of pain."

"Much better than that dancing master who tried to flirt with you." Liza winked at Greville.

Cassandra perked up. "He did, didn't he? Poor man. Did he ever get another position?"

"*I* heard he tried to elope with a young lady. Her grandfather used his cane on him."

"Rissa, wherever do you hear such things?"

Successfully distracted from their panic, the sisters entered the hall. Their mother trailed them, faintly remonstrating that gossip over an elopement was not a proper subject for debutantes.

The dowager had joined them for the Season. Wise Liza had

mentioned a fortnight before their departure that the elder Mrs. Myers would enjoy London. His mother had protested that her many activities prevented any extended absence from the village. Within a week, though, she had packed her bags and was demanding that it was time to leave. Once in London, she and her daughters became caught by the delight of shopping and fittings and planning and visiting, everything necessary for a successful season. Their joy increased as they attended their first parties, the excitements of their second week culminating in this ball at the Earl of Buckland's residence.

Greville slipped an arm around Liza's waist and swung her to face him. "Do you know what tonight is, wife? Our first anniversary."

He didn't add that a half-year ago someone had tried to kill her. He didn't want those nightmares to re-surface. She had healed more quickly than his sisters, but he never felt healed of the terror he had experienced when he saw that cricket bat swinging for her head. He'd nearly lost her. Horror still woke him at night, and the only relief was her soft form sleeping next to him.

"Don't crush my gown," she warned even as she looped her arms around his neck.

He considered the outcry if he said they wouldn't attend this first official ball of the Season. His mother had secured the invitations. She would be appalled if they didn't attend. His sisters would never forgive him.

Still, he offered. "Will this evening be too much? Hours of standing. Dancing round and round. A whole season of this. You were sick this morning and yesterday."

"It's only a little morning sickness. Mercy says to keep food in my tummy, and I'll be fine." Eyes bright, she tiptoed, and he obeyed her request.

"They're kissing again!" Cassandra stomped her foot.

Greville lifted his head and shared a chuckle with his wife.

"Come on, or we will be late," Clarissa urged.

"Late is fashionable," he told his sister then indulged himself with another of his wife's kisses.

Thank You*!*

Thank you for reading *The Key with Hearts*. Writing this book was pure pleasure. Words flew onto the page almost faster than I could get them down. I wish all of my stories flew so quickly.

In this book I mentioned the death of Greville's brother Stanton Myers, ten years before. His death is only one element in the novel *The Dangers to Hearts*. Take your chance at solving Stanton's murder, then share your thoughts with me at winkbooks@aol.com.

For any questions, comments, and speculations, please contact winkbooks@aol.com. You can find my books on my publishing website, www.writersinkbooks.com You can follow my occasional blog at maleebooks.blogspot.com. Sign up for my newsletter to receive advance notice of releases.

Indie writers thrive on reviews. With *any* book that you enjoy, please share with other readers who are looking for escape from the stresses of life.

Dream it. Believe it. Do it.
~~ M. A. Lee

Hearts in Hazard

Mysteries and Suspense with a Dash of Romance
In the Regency Era of England

1 ~ *A Game of Secrets* ~ Smugglers, secrets and spies: Kate tries to hide in plain sight; Tony tries to catch a spy. First they fall in love, then they fall into trouble with smugglers. Will they survive?

2 ~ *A Game of Spies* ~ Salons and soirées, flirtation and dancing, gambling and spies: Josette and Giles fall in love over a deck of cards—and try not to die.
Spymaster Giles Hargreaves was introduced in *A Game of Secrets*.

3 ~ *A Game of Hearts* ~ **Two couples** :: One titled widow, one wealthy businessman: two hearts shadowed by their past. One bright young flirt, one hard-edged young man: two hearts crossed by circumstance. Mix in a courtesan and two rakes, all out for mischief, and murder bloody and foul.

4 ~ *The Danger of Secrets* ~ Deep in the wintry countryside, a house warmed by relatives and friends: secrets of family, secrets of hearts, secrets of blood and pain. Match a daughter to an unknown father; match a spinster to an earl; match a serial killer to his next victim.
Gordon Musgrove was introduced in *A Game of Spies*.

5 ~ *The Danger for Spies* ~ Impossibilities? Rakes don't lose their hearts. Spies don't give up the game. No one hides in plain sight. Codes are unbreakable. A man can't hold onto revenge for years and years. Impossibilities are designed to be shattered.
Toby Kennitt was introduced in *A Game of Spies*.

6 ~ *The Danger to Hearts* ~ A country manor in early Spring: older woman and younger man. Horses, cats, needlework, roses and afternoon teas ~ What could possibly go wrong in an idyll? Trouble in the past, trouble now, and murder.
The character Jess Carter was introduced in *A Game of Secrets*.

7 ~ *The Key to Secrets* ~ Debutantes should snare fiancés, not murder them. Constable Hector Evans must solve three murders. Is his former love guilty, of is she a convenient scapegoat?

Constable Hector Evans was introduced in *The Danger to Hearts*.

8 ~ *The Key for Spies* ~ Spies and traitors. Lies and treachery. Unexpected love where bullets fly. One traitor destroys loyalty. What will two traitors destroy?

9 ~ *The Key with Hearts* ~ A convenient marriage inconveniently causes murder.

10 ~ *The Hazard of Secrets*. Two hearts with dangerous pasts— Can they keep their secrets, or will murder force them to reveal all?

11 ~ *The Hazard for Spies* ~ Disguised to spy. Will murder destroy their chance for love?

12 ~ *The Hazard for Hearts* ~ Two wives haunt the castle. Will she be the third to die?

Into Death Series, set after World War I

Digging into Death ~ A governess seeking refuge, a handsome young man, an archaeological dig: romance is inevitable; murder is not. Suspicions escalate, artifacts are stolen, and then a second murder. Has the love of her life beguiled her straight into death? Available in paperback and e-book

Christmas with Death ~ Christmas is for miracles, merriment, and murder. Set in 1919 at an English country manor for a party throughout Christmastide. Available in paperback and e-book.

Portrait with Death, publishing soon ~ the conclusion of the Isabella Newcombe series

Nonfiction by M.A. Lee

Think like a Pro Writer series

Think like a Pro: New Advent for Writers ~ Seven lessons to guide your growth from newbie writer to "thinking like a pro writer". Now available in paperback and e-book.

Think / Pro: A Planner for Writers ~ An undated planner with daily word counts, progress meters, project planning, and goals analysis. Paperback only. How else will you record your goals and progress?

Old Geeky Greeks: Write Stories with Ancient Techniques ~ Storytelling has its roots in the strong foundations of classical antiquity. Avoid the re-packaged "exclusive insights" and "wham-pow webinars" and return to the source, organized as a seminar in book form.

Discovering Your Novel ~ a 52-week course for new writers, offering guidance from original idea to publication and marketing.

Discovering Characters ~ Delving deeply into your primary characters entails more than just templates and character interviews. You also need to know your secondary characters. Focus on more than appearance, more than intellect, and explore your characters hearts and souls. Discover them!

Discovering Your Plot ~ What writers need and want for plot structures and genre expectations. Control pacing, tension, and suspense with a stronger comprehension of the major sections of a novel.

Discovering your Author Brand ~ The greatest secret to catch the attention of fly-by readers? Branding. Writers need to brand their books, their series, and themselves as the author. Packed with examples and explanations from past successful marketing efforts.

Discovering Sentence Craft ~ Zeug-what? Chiasmus? Auxesis? Are those spelled correctly? Well, yes. These are literary devices used for centuries by the best writers to make their works memorable. Writers are artists, seeking ideas from the creative muse. We're also crafters, looking for the best ways to present those creative ideas. *DiscS~Craft* presents techniques for using figurative & interpretive concepts as well as the structures of inversions, repetitions, oppositions, and sequencings.

Just Start Writing :: Inspiration 4 Writers, book 1 ~Writing can be a dizzy whirl of a carousel, all colors and mirrors with unicorns and griffins and dragons to ride. How do you get your ticket, climb on the carousel, and join the writing ride? If you want to pursue your writing dream, *Just Start Writing* will help you start.

Pen Names of M.A. Lee

Remi Black ~ Fae Mark'd

Fae Mark'd Wizard

Weave a Wizardry Web

Dream a Deadly Dream

Sing a Graveyard Song

Kindle a Fae's Wrath (coming soon)

Quench a Dragon's Fire (in the sketching stage)

Dance to Bone-Edged Music (in the sketching stage)

Fae Mark'd World

To Wield the Wind :: Spells of Air 1

To Charm the Air: Spells of Air 2 (coming soon)

To Curse the Wyre: Spells of Air 3 (sketching stage)

Edie Roones ~ Seasons in Sansward

Summer Sieges

Autumn Spells

Winter Sorcery

Spring Magicks (in the sketching stage)

. ~ . ~ . ~ .

All books from Writers' Ink are available at online distributors.

For any comments, questions, and speculations, contact
winkbooks@aol.com.
Use the subject line to direct your email to a specific book or series.

Thank You*!*

www.ingramcontent.com/pod-product-compliance
Lightning Source LLC
Chambersburg PA
CBHW020337260626
47156CB00004B/1564